Bo[lan ...]
han[gar ...]

"Give me a hand!" he shouted to the cop who'd driven him to the hangar. Together they put their weight against a rolling cast-iron engine hoist, shoving the contraption toward the door. Chains rattled and wheels creaked as the half-ton hoist rolled across the grease-stained floor, picking up momentum. The door was solid-cored oak, but neither it nor the dead bolt could hold up against the force. With a deafening crunch, the door splintered open, even as the bolt sheared through the jamb.

Bolan shoved the hoist the rest of the way into the office, using it for cover. The man inside fired twice with his automatic, bouncing slugs off the hoist, then tossed his weapon aside and threw his arms up in surrender.

The Executioner kept his Beretta trained on the man as he moved forward. "You know why we're here. Talk fast, and when your lips move they better be telling the truth."

MACK BOLAN®
The Executioner

#257 Precision Play
#258 Target Lock
#259 Nightfire
#260 Dayhunt
#261 Dawnkill
#262 Trigger Point
#263 Skysniper
#264 Iron Fist
#265 Freedom Force
#266 Ultimate Price
#267 Invisible Invader
#268 Shattered Trust
#269 Shifting Shadows
#270 Judgment Day
#271 Cyberhunt
#272 Stealth Striker
#273 UForce
#274 Rogue Target
#275 Crossed Borders
#276 Leviathan
#277 Dirty Mission
#278 Triple Reverse
#279 Fire Wind
#280 Fear Rally
#281 Blood Stone
#282 Jungle Conflict
#283 Ring of Retaliation
#284 Devil's Army
#285 Final Strike
#286 Armageddon Exit
#287 Rogue Warrior
#288 Arctic Blast
#289 Vendetta Force
#290 Pursued
#291 Blood Trade
#292 Savage Game
#293 Death Merchants
#294 Scorpion Rising

#295 Hostile Alliance
#296 Nuclear Game
#297 Deadly Pursuit
#298 Final Play
#299 Dangerous Encounter
#300 Warrior's Requiem
#301 Blast Radius
#302 Shadow Search
#303 Sea of Terror
#304 Soviet Specter
#305 Point Position
#306 Mercy Mission
#307 Hard Pursuit
#308 Into the Fire
#309 Flames of Fury
#310 Killing Heat
#311 Night of the Knives
#312 Death Gamble
#313 Lockdown
#314 Lethal Payload
#315 Agent of Peril
#316 Poison Justice
#317 Hour of Judgment
#318 Code of Resistance
#319 Entry Point
#320 Exit Code
#321 Suicide Highway
#322 Time Bomb
#323 Soft Target
#324 Terminal Zone
#325 Edge of Hell
#326 Blood Tide
#327 Serpent's Lair
#328 Triangle of Terror
#329 Hostile Crossing
#330 Dual Action
#331 Assault Force
#332 Slaughter House

Don Pendleton's The Executioner

SLAUGHTER HOUSE

A GOLD EAGLE BOOK FROM
WORLDWIDE

TORONTO • NEW YORK • LONDON
AMSTERDAM • PARIS • SYDNEY • HAMBURG
STOCKHOLM • ATHENS • TOKYO • MILAN
MADRID • WARSAW • BUDAPEST • AUCKLAND

If you purchased this book without a cover you should be aware that this book is stolen property. It was reported as "unsold and destroyed" to the publisher, and neither the author nor the publisher has received any payment for this "stripped book."

First edition July 2006
ISBN-13: 978-0-373-64332-5
ISBN-10:   0-373-64332-2

Special thanks and acknowledgment to
Ron Renauld for his contribution to this work.

SLAUGHTER HOUSE

Copyright © 2006 by Worldwide Library.

All rights reserved. Except for use in any review, the reproduction or utilization of this work in whole or in part in any form by any electronic, mechanical or other means, now known or hereafter invented, including xerography, photocopying and recording, or in any information storage or retrieval system, is forbidden without the written permission of the publisher, Worldwide Library, 225 Duncan Mill Road, Don Mills, Ontario, Canada M3B 3K9.

All characters in this book have no existence outside the imagination of the author and have no relation whatsoever to anyone bearing the same name or names. They are not even distantly inspired by any individual known or unknown to the author, and all incidents are pure invention.

® and TM are trademarks of the publisher. Trademarks indicated with ® are registered in the United States Patent and Trademark Office, the Canadian Trade Marks Office and in other countries.

Printed in U.S.A.

We used the smallest force, in the quickest time, in the farthest place.
—T. E. Lawrence, 1888–1935

By working solo I can go places and accomplish things that huge armies could never hope to achieve.
—Mack Bolan

THE MACK BOLAN

LEGEND

Nothing less than a war could have fashioned the destiny of the man called Mack Bolan. Bolan earned the Executioner title in the jungle hell of Vietnam.

But this soldier also wore another name—Sergeant Mercy. He was so tagged because of the compassion he showed to wounded comrades-in-arms and Vietnamese civilians.

Mack Bolan's second tour of duty ended prematurely when he was given emergency leave to return home and bury his family, victims of the Mob. Then he declared a one-man war against the Mafia.

He confronted the Families head-on from coast to coast, and soon a hope of victory began to appear. But Bolan had broken society's every rule. That same society started gunning for this elusive warrior—to no avail.

So Bolan was offered amnesty to work within the system against terrorism. This time, as an employee of Uncle Sam, Bolan became Colonel John Phoenix. With a command center at Stony Man Farm in Virginia, he and his new allies—Able Team and Phoenix Force—waged relentless war on a new adversary: the KGB.

But when his one true love, April Rose, died at the hands of the Soviet terror machine, Bolan severed all ties with Establishment authority.

Now, after a lengthy lone-wolf struggle and much soul-searching, the Executioner has agreed to enter an "arm's-length" alliance with his government once more, reserving the right to pursue personal missions in his Everlasting War.

1

Jotuwi Port, Malaysia

It was difficult to remain still with the gnats clouding around his face. When they moved in closer, drawn to the sweat trickling down his forehead, it was all he could do not to reach out and swat them away. But doing so would have tipped off his position, and the prospect of being targeted by 7.62 mm Parabellum rounds was even more daunting. So he let the pests have their way, keeping his focus on the gunman standing next to a late-model Land Rover parked at the end of a dirt road thirty yards downhill from the foliage-choked knoll providing his cover.

In the pale moonlight, Mack Bolan, aka the Executioner, could see that the man was Malay, tall and had swollen biceps extending beyond the rolled-up sleeves of his khaki shirt. Even though the sun had set more than an hour earlier, the man wore a pair of gold-framed aviator shades, and propped atop his head was a loose-fitting tan hat with a wide, soiled brim. He was armed with an AK-47 knockoff but held the rifle in one hand with seeming indifference, barrel angled at the dirt road that came to an abrupt end a few yards from the Land Rover's rear bumper. The vehicle had turned around shortly after reaching the dead end and was now, like the man standing alongside it, facing toward the dull glow of lights emanating from Jotuwi Port. Bolan knew the man wasn't alone. The Malay didn't match the description of Dato Jamal, an older man who served as chief customs officer for the Jotuwi Port Authority. Bolan figured Jamal was driving the Rover, waiting for a second vehicle to make its way down the dirt road before he showed himself.

Based on snatches from recent cell phone conversations intercepted by intelligence officers for the UN International Maritime Organization, Bolan also knew that Jamal's rendezvous was with some faction of the Chinese underworld. Most likely it was one of the triads whose criminal influence in recent years had spread like a bleak plague from their festering points of origin in Hong Kong and mainland China. Once the other car showed up, the Executioner would get a firsthand glimpse of who exactly had offered Jamal the equivalent of a quarter million U.S. dollars to bypass the security inspection of one particular cargo container still resting in the hold of one of the dozen or more freighters moored in the nearby harbor. The container in question held a seemingly benign shipment of industrial equipment manifested as parts for a waste filtration system. The intel Bolan received when he'd arrived in Malaysia earlier in the day told a different story, however. According to that intelligence—which included the cell phone transcripts as well as six months of undercover work by the IMO's Enforcement and Intervention Division—in the right hands the mechanical gear could be transformed into components for a two-stage countercurrent centrifuge capable of producing weapons-grade uranium.

"Somebody out there is looking to whip up some black-market nukes," Bolan had been told during his briefing by EID agent Anthony Tetlock, who was positioned farther down the road in a camouflaged Hummer that would roll out of the brush once the second vehicle passed by, boxing in Jamal and his co-conspirators. Bolan's mission had been just as succinctly spelled out by Hal Brognola, head of the U.S. Sensitive Operations Group, when he'd asked the Executioner to serve as point man for the UN force.

Bolan recalled the big Fed's exact words. "We've got to nip this in the bud, Striker."

Bolan was more than ready to do the nipping, but at the moment the ball was in the enemy's court.

DATO JAMAL FINISHED his cigarette and stubbed it out in the dashboard ashtray, then checked his watch. It was five minutes past the designated rendezvous time.

"What's keeping them?" he muttered irritably, thumping his fist against the steering wheel of the Land Rover.

The customs official had no idea what was concealed in the shipping container he was being asked to let through Jotuwi Port without being inspected. He didn't much care. Another three weeks until he retired, and this would be just one more under-the-counter transaction he'd used to swell the nest egg that would allow him to live comfortably into his later years.

Dealing with thugs had never been something he enjoyed, but a government pension went only so far. There was no way he was going to end up like other retired civil servants living on cat food and handouts from pitying relatives.

As another minute ticked off his watch, Jamal fought back a nagging sense that perhaps he'd gone too far when he'd upped his price for looking the other way when approached with a smuggling proposition. What if they'd decided to shrug him off and try to sneak their container through the port without his assistance? It wouldn't be that difficult, he thought. After all, Jotuwi Port, on average, ran security screens on less than a quarter of the cargo passing through its harbor. With any luck, the contraband could slip through the cracks without the Chinese having to pay him off. If it came to that, he could blow the whistle on them, but doing so would open himself up to incrimination as well.

Another concern gnawing at Jamal was that the Chinese had decided to make him pay for upping his fee. The customs officer had come to this remote spot for payoffs numerous times without incident, but who was to say the Chinese wouldn't take advantage of the setup and decide to teach him a lesson?

The prospect hadn't just dawned on Jamal. He'd taken it into consideration and made the necessary arrangements to protect himself. Peering in the rearview mirror, the customs official eyed the shadowy figures huddled in the back of the SUV. The four men, armed with assault rifles, would be ready to deal with any problems that might arise.

Jamal checked his watch again.

"You want to play games with me?" he grumbled, staring down the still empty road. "Fine, let's play games."

THE LONGER HE WAITED for the rendezvous, the more Bolan became aware of all the sounds filtering through the seeming quiet. Unseen birds chirped and cawed up high in the treetops, where agile-limbed proboscis monkeys could also be heard shrieking their way through a network of intertwining limbs and branches. Throngs of insects, clearly much larger and louder than the gnats, buzzed their way through the lower elevations. Still more wildlife could be heard splashing about in a nearby tributary screened from Bolan's view by the verdant overgrowth. En route to his position, Bolan had nearly tumbled into the brackish waterway, which ran parallel to the road and extended from the harbor deep into the heart of the jungle. The water stunk of effluent, and Bolan could still smell the fetid stench over the scent of tropical flowers.

Minutes passed. The gnats had mercifully tired of Bolan and flitted off in search of other sustenance. Relieved of their torment, the Executioner shifted his weight slightly to ease a cramping in his right arm and allow greater mobility to his gun hand, which was clenched around a Beretta 93-R fitted with a customized three-inch sound suppressor. His left hand was curled around the pistol's folding foregrip for increased accuracy, but at this range Bolan felt confident that, if need be, he could hit his target single-handed.

Finally there was a change in the tableau that lay downhill from Bolan. The driver's window of the Land Rover slipped open and there was an exchange of words between the gunner and the man behind the wheel. Bolan had been right: Jamal was the driver.

The gunman nodded, then quietly sauntered to the back of the Land Rover and swung open the rear door. Watching, Bolan stiffened. Four men spilled out of the back of the SUV, each one armed with a clone AK-47 similar to that carried by the man who'd just turned them loose. The Executioner let out a quick breath and nestled his index finger closer to the Beretta's trigger.

He'd already thumbed the firing selector for 3-round bursts. He was ready to fire at the first indication the men were onto him, but their movements suggested the men had some other agenda on their minds. Not so much as a single glance had been cast his way, and when the men fanned out, they moved away from him, taking up positions in the nearby brush.

Ambush, Bolan thought to himself. The Malays were clearly intent on bushwhacking whoever was coming to meet with them. This wasn't the way Bolan had figured on things playing out, but at this point there was little he could do about it. There was a walkie-talkie clipped to his waist that could put him in contact with Tetlock and the commandos riding with him in the Humvee. But with the enemy lurking in the nearby brush, he wasn't about to draw attention to himself by reaching for the communicator, much less speaking into it.

Once the ambushers were in position, the original Malay rifleman ambled casually back to his position alongside the driver's side of the Rover. He fished through his shirt pocket for a pack of cigarettes and tapped out two, one for himself, the other for Jamal. He was lighting up when, in the distance, there was a sudden flurry of faint poping sounds, followed by several louder blasts. The rifleman let out an exclamation and flicked his cigarette aside, looking down the road in the direction of the port. Jamal likewise shouted out in Malay, his voice carrying into the surrounding jungle. Bolan didn't know the language, but he had a good idea what the men were up in arms about.

Something was going down in the harbor. The ambush was off.

Or so they thought.

The Land Rover's engine roared to life as the gunmen scurried from hiding and jogged back to the road. They were filing back into the SUV when Bolan suddenly heard a droning sound, high-pitched, coming from the tributary to his right. He was trying to pinpoint the exact location of the sound when everything was drowned out by the fevered chatter of what sounded to Bolan like rounds from a large-caliber machine gun.

The Land Rover was the target. High-powered rounds bored into the vehicle's siding, punctuated by the shattering of glass and the agonized cries of those strafed by the fusillade. The tables had been turned on the ambushers. Caught off guard, three of the gunmen tumbled from the vehicle and were dead by the time they hit the ground. A fourth Malay reached out from inside the SUV and swung the door closed while the remaining rifleman—the same man who'd first sounded the alarm—dropped to his knees, mortally wounded, peppering the jungle with errant return fire.

Jamal had apparently been hit as well, because after lurching down the road a few dozen yards, the Land Rover abruptly swerved off course and crashed headlong into the unyielding trunk of a decades-old banyan tree. The engine died and the vehicle's horn began to blare. Through the shattered windows, Bolan could see Dato Jamal slumped lifelessly over the wheel. The other man inside the vehicle staggered out, only to be mowed down by yet another onslaught from unseen forces.

The Malays had been beaten at their own game, the Executioner realized. He figured there was no point in waiting for the double-crossers to show themselves. If he wanted to find out who they were, he was going to have to track them down to the spot where they'd staged their counterambush.

Rising, Bolan crouched low, both hands still on his Beretta, and quickly stole through the snarl of vegetation around him, retracing his steps to the reeking river. The high-pitched drone he'd heard earlier grew louder. Once he reached the water's edge, Bolan could make out the shadowy outline of a hydrofoil in the middle of the river.

There were three men aboard the small craft. One was armed with an assault rifle. Another was poised behind a machine gun mounted near the man operating the hydrofoil's controls. Judging from their bulky headgear, Bolan guessed the men had relied on night-vision goggles for the deadly accuracy of their ambush. When the boat abruptly changed course and veered toward the embankment where he was standing, the Executioner further surmised that at least one pair of those goggles was trained on him.

Seconds later, the air around Bolan was alive with fired rounds packing the kind of deadly sting gnats could only dream about....

2

The most common fatal mistake made by an unseasoned warrior was to be caught flat-footed in the face of incoming fire. In his time, Bolan had seen many good soldiers freeze in their tracks once they realized the enemy had the drop on them. And in nearly every such instance the ultimate price was paid for that moment's hesitation. That Bolan himself had eluded such a fate was a tribute to instincts honed by years of combat, and those instincts kicked in the moment the Executioner saw the hydrofoil gunners drawing bead on him.

Even as his would-be assailants were triggering their first rounds, Bolan was on the move, pushing off to his right and spinning sharply, making himself an elusive target. As bullets chewed through the foliage where he'd been standing a split second earlier, he was hurtling over the thick trunk of a long-toppled mangrove that sloped down into the murky water. The trunk was sodden with decay but still firm enough to blunt the pummeling gunfire.

Once he'd inched forward a few yards, the Executioner rose just enough to brace himself for a two-handed shot at the enemy. The muzzle-flash of the M-60 mounted behind the front seat of the hydrofoil gave him an easy target, and the Beretta recoiled in his palm as it sent a 3-round burst burrowing into the gunner's chest. By the time the other gunman had shifted aim and triggered a return volley, Bolan had spun, taking himself out of the line of fire.

It was a nimble, life-saving maneuver, but it came at a price, as Bolan's right foot slid into a narrow gap between the tree trunk and the aqueous mud that lined the embankment. It was as if unseen hands had suddenly reached out and locked Bolan's ankle in a death grip. When he tried to pull his leg free of the muck, the suction increased. The soldier cursed under his breath. He was pinned beneath the toppled tree, with the enemy closing in.

He could hear the hydrofoil slowing as it neared the embankment. More rounds from the surviving gunner's assault rifle burrowed into the spongy pulp of the decaying mangrove. As long as Bolan remained trapped, all his attacker would have to do was keep firing until the steady stream of bullets gouged through the dead wood to its intended target.

Bolan, however, wasn't about to let that happen. Steeling himself, he leaned back and extended his right arm fully, then raised it above the trunk and fired blindly at the watercraft. It was merely a diversion, and it worked, as the enemy rifleman quickly redirected his aim toward the source of the shot.

By then, Bolan had pulled back and was sitting up, well out of harm's way. He'd bought himself a few precious seconds, and he put them to good use, sizing up the hydrofoil. Left hand secured on the Beretta's foregrip, he took aim, this time not at the gunner, but rather the man at the boat's controls.

Another 3-round burst spit forth from the Beretta. One bullet clanged off the hydrofoil's rear-mounted fan blades, but the other two found flesh and bone. The boat's operator groaned, then, like the driver of the ill-fated Land Rover, he died at the controls. Just as the SUV had swerved off the road and smashed into a tree, the hydrofoil, engine still running, quickly strayed off its mid-river course and veered toward the outermost branches of the half-submerged tree Bolan was pinned beneath.

Bolan braced himself.

The moment the boat struck the tree, he flexed his right

ankle. As he'd hoped, the impact was strong enough to jar the trunk, briefly displacing the mud that had enveloped his foot. Focusing his strength, the Executioner yanked his leg upward, wresting it free of the muck. A sharp twinge burned through his right hamstring. Bolan ignored the pain and rolled clear of the tree trunk, ready to contend with the surviving rifleman. He was hoping the force of the collision might have thrown the man off balance into the snarl of tree branches that lay above the waterline.

No such luck.

Beretta poised in both hands, the Executioner eyed the hydrofoil. Now silent, the boat lay tangled in the tree limbs, and aboard the trapped craft he could see the two men he'd slain earlier. There was no sign of the third assailant.

Bolan rose to a crouch, peering beyond the boat. In the moonlight he could see clots of foam riding small crests in the river current. A shift in the breeze stung his nostrils with the smell of raw pollutants. Overhead, the jungle canopy had turned into a shriekfest as birds and monkeys alike were reacting to the exchange of gunfire.

Moments later, Bolan heard a telltale splashing out in the river. He tracked the sound to the far bank, just in time to spot a man pulling himself from the water. He'd left his night-vision headgear in the river, and his shaved head gleamed faintly in the moonlight.

Bolan took aim and shouted for the man to stop, but his warning went unheeded. Once the other man had a footing on the embankment, he lurched from side to side, weaving his way up the muddy slope. Bolan emptied his magazine, firing figure eights in hope the man would zigzag into the line of fire. If any of the rounds found their target, they didn't take the man down. In a matter of seconds, he'd vanished from view into the dense shelter of the Malaysian jungle.

Bolan grabbed a fresh 20-round magazine from the ammo clip on his belt. As he reloaded, he gauged the strength of the polluted current separating him from his prey. Even without his strained hamstring, he knew it was pointless to try swimming across the tributary. By the time he reached the other side, the man would be long gone, provided he didn't double back to the riverbank, in which case he'd be able to gun Bolan down while he was in the water. Freeing the hydrofoil from the tree limbs would be time-consuming as well, and there was no guarantee he could get the boat running.

No, giving chase was not an option. At least not for the moment.

Fighting back his frustration, Bolan angrily grabbed the walkie-talkie clipped next to his ammo pack. Much as the Executioner preferred tackling assignments on his own, there were times when the only option was to call in reinforcements. He assumed Tetlock, alerted by the gunfire, was en route in the Hummer. Bolan keyed the palm-sized transceiver. Once he received a response, he wearily gave his position and voiced the three words he was most loath to speak while on a mission.

"I need backup."

3

Field Agent Anthony Tetlock of the UN Maritime Organization clicked off his headset and turned to Mack Bolan, shaking his head.

"No sign of him," Tetlock reported, passing along the update he'd just received from aerial spotters aboard the three OH-58D Kiowa Warriors helicopters combing the jungle terrain into which Bolan's mystery assailant had fled following the crash of the hydrofoil. Bolan could see two of the choppers in the distance, probing the ground below with high-powered searchlights.

Bolan and Tetlock were standing near the embankment where the shootout had taken place. Less than an hour had passed since the altercation, but the area was already swarming with response teams. Local paramedics and coroner officials were tending to the dead. They'd bagged those gunned down in the earlier ambush involving the Land Rover and were now retrieving the slain gunners aboard the crashed hydrofoil. Three of Tetlock's colleagues with the UNMO's Enforcement and Intervention Division were scouring both scenes. Wearing latex gloves and lighting their way with club-sized flashlights, the men were looking more for evidence than clues, as they had already managed to piece together what had happened, not only in the jungle but back in the harbor.

Bolan had just learned that the intended buyers of the contraband centrifuges were members of the Free Aceh separatist movement looking for increased firepower in their yearslong battle to secede from the Republic of Indonesia. The news had taken Bolan by surprise, because a band of his colleagues—the Stony Man commando force known as Phoenix Force—were on assignment in Aceh trying to track down members of the same insurgent force for their role in a car-bombing that had claimed the life of three U.S. citizens on a fact-finding mission for Amnesty International.

The separatists involved in the centrifuge transaction had pirated the small freighter they'd brought to Jotuwi Port. Those same forces had opened fire in the harbor once they realized they were being shadowed by a waterborne EID strike force. The UN commandos had returned fire and stormed the craft, killing eleven separatists and taking two into custody while freeing the original crew. The sounds of that abbreviated firefight had triggered the bloodbath in the jungle.

"We don't have any proof yet," Tetlock said, scratching the stubble on his chin as he and Bolan stared at the slain victims of the ambush, "but my guess is the Chinese probably cut a separate deal with another port official who could be bribed for less money, then decided to whack Jamal once they got word the transaction had been made. When they heard all hell breaking loose in the harbor, they must've figured they'd been double-crossed and decided to take it out on Jamal and his goons."

"I guess that makes sense," Bolan said. "Of course, once they saw that Jamal was planning an ambush of his own, I think there was going to be a shootout regardless."

"Whatever the case, I'll take the bad guys killing each other any time."

"I second that," Bolan said. "But in this case I had to lend a hand."

"Not to mention a hamstring," Tetlock said, glancing down at the leg Bolan was favoring. "Maybe you ought to sit down and take a load off."

"I'm fine," Bolan said.

The Executioner watched as the two bodies were removed from the hydrofoil and hauled ashore.

"Hold on," Tetlock called out to the medics placing the victims on twin stretchers laid out on the embankment. "I want a better look at these guys."

Bolan limped slightly as he followed the UN official over to the bodies. Both men were Chinese, probably in their early twenties. They were nondescript in appearance save for their bullet wounds and tattoos. In the case of the latter, each man's right forearm was inked with an elaborately detailed image of a fire-breathing dragon whose tail wrapped around his wrist and extended to the back of his hand, which was additionally inked with Chinese script.

"They're triad, all right," Bolan murmured, knowing that such tattoos were part of an initiation rite for those joining the ranks of one of the world's most feared crime organizations.

"San Hop Kwan," Tetlock added, pointing to the lettering on the men's hands. "Last I checked, they were at the top of the pecking order back in Hong Kong. Used to be they were content with the vice rackets, but lately they've ratcheted things up a notch or two."

"Peddling nukes seems like more than just a couple notches," Bolan said.

"Maybe so," Tetlock conceded. "And the thing is, I've got a feeling we've just scratched the tip of the iceberg."

A MILE UPRIVER from where Mack Bolan and Anthony Tetlock were ruminating over his slain colleagues, Jiang Yang clung desperately to the lower lip of an algae-lined concrete pipe discharging a thick, opaque spew of liquid factory waste into the same tributary he'd earlier traveled by hydrofoil. The triad gangster was back in the water, submerged up to his chin with his arms fully extended upward, holding on to the pipe.

The effluent cascaded directly over him, shielding him from view of those aboard the Kiowa Warrior hovering some fifty yards above the current.

Yang held his breath as best he could, wary of ingesting any of the pollutants coursing off his head and splashing off the back of his neck. Given the noxious smell, he was worried that the sewage might kill him just as surely as sniper rounds from enemy gunners in the overhead chopper.

The glare of the Kiowa's searchlight streaked across the surface of the water, inching closer to the discharge spout, one of three such conduits disgorging waste from the Malaysia National Rubber Plant, a four-building complex resting on seven acres of land carved out of the nearby jungle. Yang wasn't sure how much longer he could he could hold on to the pipe. He'd lost feeling in both hands and was relying on sheer willpower to keep from losing his grip and dropping into the river.

When the shaft of light fell upon the conduit, Yang forced himself to remain still. The beam rested on the outpouring of sewage for a seeming eternity, then finally drifted away from Yang and trailed up the embankment to the perimeter fence encircling the rubber plant.

Yang waited until he could hear the Kiowa floating away from the river, then spit sewage from his lips and drew in a deep breath. He let go of the discharge pipe and dropped back into the tainted water. Eyes closed, holding his breath, Yang swam beneath the waterline, making his way toward the opposite embankment. Once he felt as if his lungs were about to burst, he broke to the surface and quietly dogpaddled the last few yards to the riverbank. There, exhausted, he pulled himself from the water and crawled to the concealment of some thick bushes, then collapsed, retching violently.

The stench of raw effluent clung to him, and even after he'd vomited everything in his system he remained nauseous and weak in the knees. He wanted nothing more than to scrub himself raw beneath a scalding shower, spoon down some soup hot and spicy enough to burn off the river residue clinging to the inside of his mouth, then pass out for a good twelve hours between the clean sheets of a warm bed. But Yang knew it would be some time before he could indulge himself with such amenities. He may have eluded his pursuers for the moment, but he also knew he was a long way from being rid of them. He needed to find a way out of the jungle and back to the outskirts of Jotuwi. He hoped several of his San Hop Kwan colleagues were still holed up in a remote safehouse near the private airfield Yang and his slain underlings had landed at earlier in the week when they'd come to oversee the sale of their centrifuges.

As for that transaction, the moment he heard gunfire in the harbor, his guess had been that the deal had been thwarted, which meant that even if he did escape his present dilemma, he would still have an ordeal ahead of him.

There were those within the triad hierarchy who'd warned him from day one that it was a mistake to traffic in nuclear materials. *"Stay with what we know best,"* they'd told him. *"Why mess with a good thing?"*

Eager to carve out a niche for himself, Yang had ignored the warnings. After all, he'd thought, he was using the same procedures and same contacts to peddle nukes that he had moving drugs. *What was the difference?* he'd figured. Looking back, he realized he should have been more on his guard the moment Dato Jamal had upped his fee. He should have taken it for a sign. Yes, he'd had the last laugh on the customs official, but at what price? Two of his best men had just been slain, and a few million dollars' worth of equipment had been likely confiscated along with the tenfold profit he'd hoped to make on the deal. His plan had been to return to Hong Kong a bona fide player, not only in the eyes of his fellow Dai Los, but also the old guard. Instead, he'd be returning with egg on his face. Provided, of course, that he managed to return at all.

Soon Yang could no longer hear the search choppers. The feeling had come back to his fingers, so he propped himself up and struggled to his feet, all the while pondering his next move. Slowly he began to make his way through the foliage that lined the embankment. Up ahead he could see a footbridge extending across the river from the rubber plant to a large clearing that had been turned into a parking lot for the workers who could afford their own transportation. Earlier, Yang had seen the Kiowa set down in the parking lot, allowing a handful of men to disembark long enough to search the cars and perimeter. He doubted they would double back for another inspection. Still, he knew he would have to proceed swiftly.

Yang took heart when he reached the lot and found it deserted saved for the parked vehicles. He began going from car to car, searching for one with unlocked doors and keys in the ignition. It quickly became apparent, however, that he was not about to be so easily accommodated. He amended his search to older model cars that would be easier to break into and hotwire. He settled on a battered gray Yugo with tinted windows that he figured would help shield him from view once he got behind the wheel. The car had been in a collision, and both doors on the driver's side were caved in several inches, leaving gaps in both the door and window frames.

"Perfect," Yang murmured to himself, reaching to his side.

The gangster had lost both his assault rifle and Walther pistol in the river somewhere near the hydrofoil, but still clipped to his waist was his prized fighting chain. Made of seven straight, flattened strips of hard-forged steel linked by interlocking rings, the weapon could be employed as anything from a whip to the whirling equivalent of martial-arts nunchaku.

Yang put the chain to new use, slipping one of the end strips into the gap in the front door, then wriggling it back and forth to trip the lock. When the mechanism wouldn't cooperate, Yang cursed and withdrew the chain. He was about to reinsert it at a different angle when he detected motion out on the footbridge.

Ducking behind the Yugo, Yang peered out toward the river and saw one of the plant workers making his way across the bridge toward the parking lot. The man was alone. Sensing opportunity, Yang's hopes rallied.

Once the plant worker cleared the bridge, he yawned his way to the parking lot, fishing through his rumpled trousers for his keys. His car was faded silver Tercel parked a few spots away from the Yugo.

Yang remained crouched as he quietly circled the crumpled import, wrapping opposite ends of the fighting chain around both hands to create a makeshift garrote. He waited until the other man was fitting his key into the Tercel, then made his move.

The worker sensed motion behind him, but by the time he turned around, Yang was already upon him. The chain-linked steel strips swiftly encircled the man's neck, strangling his cry of alarm. Yang kneed the man in the groin and slipped behind him, all the while tightening the chain. There was a brief struggle, but the worker never had a chance. Gasping, arms flailing, the man sagged to his knees, face turning crimson, then blue. His eyes bulged, filled with terror. Then, at the same time the fight went out of him, his gaze turned lifeless.

Yang gave a final tug, then lowered his victim to the ground and loosened the chain from around his neck. He took the man's keys before dragging him into the nearby brush, making certain he would remain undetected by anyone coming into the parking lot. Less than thirty seconds later, the Tercel groaned to life and Yang pulled out of the parking lot, heading down the two-lane dirt road that led back to Jotuwi.

4

Stony Man Farm, Virginia

While Jiang Yang negotiated his way through jungle back roads in the dead of the Malaysian night, half a world away the early-afternoon sun shone brightly on the base headquarters for the Sensitive Operations Group America's top counterterrorism teams. Stony Man Farm, nestled in a remote niche of the Blue Ridge Mountains, was a vast sprawl of planted fields, blooming orchards and tracts of fast-growing poplar trees destined to be turned into lumber and wood chips at the estate's small-scale timber mill. The steady agricultural output went a long way toward convincing neighboring owners throughout the Shenandoah Valley that Stony Man Farm was a purely commercial enterprise

This day, Hal Brognola had arrived directly from a meeting with the President of the United States. The primary topic of conversation had been increased piracy in the South China Sea and the risk it posed in terms of sensitive materials falling into the hands of black marketeers and, ultimately, forces with terrorist designs on the United States. The urgent meeting had been called after word was received of the incident at Jotuwi Port.

"For once, we didn't have to hard sell the skeptics," Brognola told Barbara Price, Stony Man's mission controller, as he briefed her on the meeting. "When you speculate a worst-case scenario, then get a news flash that it's just been played out, it's hard for people to call you an alarmist."

"On the bright side," Price countered, "in this case the contraband was intercepted before it changed hands. We dodged a bullet."

"For now, maybe," Brognola said. "But who's to say while we were nabbing perps in Malaysia some other transaction wasn't going down in some other port? Hell, it could turn out that whole thing in Jotuwi was just a diversionary ploy."

"Not a comforting thought," Price conceded. "In any event, we've let Phoenix Force know what happened. No word yet on whether the separatists captured in Jotuwi are the same ones behind that car-bombing they're looking into."

"There has to be a connection," Brognola insisted. "From all the intel I've looked at, they're a tight-knit batch. The right hand always knows what the left's doing."

"I suspect we'll find out soon enough."

Brognola and Price fell silent as they made their way to the Computer Room in the Annex, where Aaron Kurtzman, Carmen Delahunt and Akira Tokaido were, as usual, plumbing the depths of cyberspace in search of data to help the Farm's field teams better carry out their missions.

Tokaido had downloaded a Satcam link filled with aerial views of Malaysia's Jotuwi Port and the surrounding peninsula. Although the Japanese-American cyberwizard had no way of knowing it yet, the images, taken over the past two hours, included a shot of the Malaysian National Rubber Plant taken less than two minutes after Jiang Yang had carjacked the Toyota Tercel.

But Yang hadn't completely slipped under the cybercrew's radar. Once Brognola had briefed Kurtzman on his White House meeting and asked for an update on the situation in Jotuwi Port, Kurtzman explained that he'd run a background check on the Hong Kong gangsters Bolan had slain in the tributary waters leading to the harbor. By process of elimination, he was almost certain he'd pinpointed the triad member who'd managed to get away.

"His name is Jiang Yang," Kurtzman reported, drawing Brognola's and Price's attention to his computer monitor, which was filled with a downloaded police mug shot of a Chinese man in his midtwenties. Yang was scowling at the camera with a sullen gaze devoid of any sense of humanity. His head was shaved, as were his eyebrows and any facial hair.

"They call him Skull Face, as if you couldn't guess," Kurtzman said, pausing to lean past his workstation for fresh coffee. As he grabbed the nearby carafe, he glanced up from his wheelchair at Price and Brognola. They both shook their heads.

"No, thanks," Brognola deadpanned. "I've got a few miles left before I need the oil changed."

"Fuming," Kurtzman replied with a grin, lofting his cup. "Nothing like a good cup of 10W30 to keep the gearbox lubed."

Price had heard Kurtzman's entire repertoire of coffee shtick more times than she cared to remember. She smiled faintly and steered Kurtzman back on track. "What's the lowdown on Yang?" she asked.

"Good question," Kurtzman responded. He sipped his coffee, then pecked at his keyboard, calling up a few split screens on the computer monitor. "Most of the early priors on his rap sheet are for petty crimes. Theft, assault, pandering…the usual crap you'd expect from a punk working his way through the ranks.

"Two years ago they got a murder charge to stick and he did some hard time," Kurtzman went on, calling up a document culled from a Hong Kong police database. "From the looks of it, for him it was like being sent to finishing school. He must've clicked with a well-placed inmate, because once he got out he wound up thick with San Hop Kwan's top banana, a guy named Hu Dzem."

"I've heard of him," Brognola said. "Bad tan, bad attitude, right?"

"That's the one," Kurtzman said. "As triad chairman, he obviously has his fingers in a lot of pies, but his meat-and-potatoes is a Hong Kong prostitution ring that caters to the well-to-do. Yang was part of an overseas procurement team."

"A pimp?" Price asked.

"More like a rustler, I'd say," Kurtzman corrected. "He was in charge of providing Dzem's brothels with 'exotics,' which in this case meant white women for Asian clients."

"Something tells me not many of these white women are volunteers," Price surmised.

"Afraid not," Kurtzman responded. "Like it or not, white slavery is alive and well."

"All right, I think it's clear this guy won't be up for Citizen of the Year any time soon," Brognola interjected, "but how do we get him from prostitution to trafficking nuke parts?"

"That one we're still working on," Kurtzman confessed. "But while we're doing that, we've cobbled together a who's who in terms of the crowd Yang runs with."

The computer expert called up a new screen filled with more than a dozen mug shots of other members of the San Hop Kwan Triad. "I'm going to forward this to Striker so he can be on the lookout for this guy's other homeys. I mean, you have to figure he went to Malaysia with more than two guys."

Brognola nodded.

"Do we have anything else?" Barbara Price asked.

"Let me see." Kurtzman glanced across the room at Akira Tokaido, who was hunched over his workstation, head bobbing to the sonic throb of music blaring through ear buds linked to his MP3 player. To get the Japanese American's attention, Kurtzman wadded a sheet of computer paper and tossed it, striking Tokaido's monitor. Tokaido glanced up as he lowered the volume on his music player.

"You rang?" he called back to Kurtzman.

"Any luck backtracking the shipment that container the centrifuges was part of?"

Tokaido nodded. "Last port of call before Jotuwi was Hainan Island," he reported.

"I thought Hainan was strictly a tourist haven," Brognola said.

"For the most part, yeah," Tokaido said, "but there are a few manufacturing plants there, too. I'm trying to find out if the centrifuge parts could've been made there. I should have something within the hour."

"Good job," Brognola said. "And if it turns out you're right, we're going to want to know who's running those factories."

"Already on it," Tokaido said. "That's part of the same search I'm running."

Kurtzman winked and gave Tokaido a thumbs-up, then said to Brognola, "Hey, did I train this guy well or what?"

Brognola quipped, "That's why we pay you the big bucks, Bear."

"Yeah, right." Kurtzman guffawed.

Price wasn't in a joking mood. She mulled over the information that had just been passed along by Kurtzman and Tokaido, and she didn't like the way it was adding up. "If we've got a triad gang turning out these centrifuge parts and selling them to the highest bidder, that's major," she intoned.

"Actually, I'll take that scenario over the other one that jumps out at me," Brognola said. When Price's gaze met his, the big Fed continued, "What if it's the Chinese government turning out these centrifuges? What if they've cut a deal with San Hop Kwan to do the wheeling and dealing for them?"

Price shook her head. "That'd be like the President putting the Mafia in charge of the Commerce Department."

"More or less," Kurtzman murmured. "That's something to keep you up nights worrying, eh?"

Two workstations over from the console where Tokaido was laboring, Carmen Delahunt glanced up from her keyboard and spoke for the first time since Brognola and Price had entered the Computer Room.

"Whoa!" she called out. "Here's a real fluke for you."

"What's that?" Price responded as she and Brognola ventured over to Delahunt's cubicle.

Carmen Delahunt had come to Stony Man by way of the FBI, but she evoked little of the stodginess associated with the Bureau. She was a middle-aged woman with vibrant red hair and a droll wit that she used as often as a rap star tossed out profanities.

"I've been sifting through Yang's résumé," Delahunt told the others. "I tried running with this theory that maybe he got moved out of prostitution because the heat was on him for one of his white slavery nabs. Bingo."

Delahunt toggled her mouse. Downloaded from the San Francisco *Daily's* online Website, was an article about media tycoon Scott Kelmin's wayward teenaged daughter, Eva, who'd been in and out of rehab for substance abuse before disappearing two months earlier.

"Little Eva," Brognola said, recalling the incident. "They thought she was a runaway at first, but wound up treating it as an abduc—" The big Fed's voice trailed off as the pieces fell into place for him. "They think she was snatched by the triad?"

"Not just that," Delahunt said, scrolling down the screen. "There was an eyewitness to her supposed abduction, and she provided a description of the perp. Guess who?"

Price and Brognola found themselves staring at a police sketch of man eerily similar to the skull-faced man depicted in the mug shot they'd eyed moments ago.

"Looks like Yang, all right," Brognola said. "But what was he doing in San Francisco?"

"Their Chinatown is the biggest San Hop Kwan affiliate

in the States," Delahunt responded. "And if you're looking for attractive white chicks to ship back home for your horn dog clients, there are worse places to look than Frisco."

5

Hong Kong

Christine Wood tucked a loose strand of hair beneath the cream-colored bandanna wrapped around her head. She was wearing a pair of large-framed glasses and a nondescript, loose-fitting jogging suit not unlike those worn by more than half the American women riding the double-decker tourist bus that had just carried them and their husbands past the glut of strip bars and hostess clubs lining Lockhart Road. As the bus turned right and started down Luard Street, the tour guide, a rotund woman with unnaturally gleaming teeth and lips the color of ripe plums, joked lamely, "I guess we better do a quick head count and make sure all of the men are still with us."

A few laughs emanated through the upper deck of the bus and several of the women elbowed their husbands. Wood glanced at the man sitting beside her and rolled her eyes.

"She never stops, does she?"

"Struggling actress, I guess," the man replied.

"Struggling is right," Wood said. "Poor twit doesn't know the difference between a joke and a jock strap."

"Now, now, honey," the man chided. "We're here to enjoy ourselves, remember? Don't go spoiling things."

Wood smiled stiffly. "Whatever you say, sweetheart."

The man was not Christine Wood's sweetheart, any more than they were there to enjoy themselves. Terrance Molvico, a native of Columbus, Ohio, was a field agent for Inter-Trieve Investigations in the Hong Kong office. He'd picked up Wood at the airport earlier in the week upon her arrival from San Francisco, and for the past two days they'd worked together chasing leads to the possible whereabouts of Eva Kelmin. Tips from informants had gotten them nowhere, but earlier that afternoon they'd had some luck showing a photo of Kelmin to street urchins haunting the back alleys of Lan Kwai Fong. Two different transients claimed to have seen Eva the previous week being escorted from a Town Car parked in front of a refurbished hotel on Hennessey Avenue. Both witnesses said that at one point Kelmin had called out for help and tried to break away from the two men ushering her into the building. No one had intervened, however, even when one of the men had backhanded the woman with enough force to knock her off her feet.

Once Molvico had run a check on the address, he'd confirmed what Wood already suspected. The hotel—the Dynasty Club—was owned by the San Hop Kwan Triad and served as a brothel for high-paying clients looking for something they couldn't find at the dives along Lockhart Road. It would have been easy enough to go to the authorities with their suspicions, but Molvico knew the triads had moles positioned deep within nearly every branch of local law enforcement. If word leaked that Kelmin had been seen at the brothel, Wood and Molvico knew the runaway would be whisked off to another location, leaving them back at square one. Like it or not, this was a matter the Inter-Trieve agents were going to have to handle on their own. On the bright side, if they could bring Eva back without assistance, the three-million-dollar reward would stay in-house, with Wood and Molvico each picking up a hefty bonus.

Once the tour bus turned left onto Hennessey Avenue, Wood opened her purse and reached past her concealed Ruger pistol for an equally sophisticated palm-sized digital camera.

"Ready?" she asked Molvico.

"Sure thing," Molvico replied. "I gotta warn you, though. I haven't learned how to say cheese in Chinese yet."

"If that's the biggest glitch we have to deal with, I'll be happy," Wood said.

Traffic was heavy in both directions. Separating the eastbound lanes from the west was a wide median strip planted with grass and a row of twenty-year-old acacia trees winking with strands of small white lights. The south side of the street was choked with small, one-story tourist shops and several taller hotels. One of the hotels, the White Orchid Inn, was located directly across from the building Eva Kelmin had reportedly been ushered into, and earlier in the day Molvico had booked a second-floor room overlooking the street. Another Inter-Trieve agent, Sam Chen, was already in the room, staking out the Dynasty.

Because the view was partially obstructed by the acacias, Wood had struck upon the idea of using a double-decker bus to get a closer look at the Dynasty's second story, where the brothel's sexual transactions were said to take place. Granted, the odds of spotting Eva were slim, but Wood figured the more information they could gather on the brothel's layout, the better their chances of freeing the teenager.

Wood and Molvico had chosen this particular tour bus because its itinerary included a brief stop between the Dynasty and an adjacent building, a stately looking, eighteenth-century Colonial manor. As the tour guide proceeded to explain, the mansion was originally the only building on the entire block and had served as the private residence for a British prefect during the years preceding the infamous Opium Wars. While the woman continued on about the house's architectural and historical significance, Molvico slid down his window and posed in front of it. Wood readied her camera and pretended to take several photos of her would-be husband. Molvico hammed it up for the benefit of the other tourists.

"I think I was blinking on that last one," he complained. "Take a couple more."

"You always blink when I take a shot," Wood teased, continuing to snap the shutter. "What is it with you, anyway?"

"Dazzled by your beauty, I guess." Molvico smirked at her. "Cheese."

Wood continued to click away, all the while aiming the camera over Molvico's shoulder and focusing on the second story of the Dynasty Club. Each room had a small balcony extending over the sidewalk, but no one was out and the shades on all the windows were drawn. There were lights on in most of the rooms, however, and through the thin shades of the second to last window she could see a man and woman standing close together in what looked to be some sort of embrace. She doubted the camera would be able to pick up much detail, but she zoomed in with the telephoto lens anyway and snapped the shutter release.

Wood continued to shoot as the bus began to pull away, managing to get a couple shots of the alleyway between the brothel and the old mansion.

"Any luck?" Molvico asked as he sat back down next to Wood.

"Not really," Wood confessed. "But I saw a fire escape in the alley that we somehow missed. That might come in handy."

"What about the balcony doors?"

"Sliders," she said. "We'll have to do blow-ups to make sure, but I think they just have conventional latch locks. Easy enough to get past."

"Except for the part about the balconies facing a street that's busy around the clock."

"Well, if we decide to go in that way, we'll try one of the back rooms, obviously," Wood countered. "That or one overlooking the alley."

"Hopefully it won't come to that," Molvico said. "I still

think our best shot is for me to play a john and go in through the front door saying I want some American tail."

"That's what I like about you," Wood said. "You're so refined."

Molvico shrugged. "Hey, they expect Americans to be crude. I go in there acting refined, it's going to raise a red flag."

"You go in there asking for a woman who matches Eva's description and they'll have plenty enough reason to be suspicious."

"Look," Molvico said, "I'll keep it vague enough that they trot out a few ladies for me to look at, okay? If Eva's there, she'll just be part of the mix. I'll hem and haw before I choose her and we'll take it from there. Any luck, her room will be close to that fire escape and we can hightail our way down to the alley. Have a car ready and vroom, we're outta there. Mission accomplished."

Wood rolled her eyes. "I tell you what," she said. "If it goes down that easy, I'll give you my share of the bounty."

"Just trying to be optimistic."

"You do that," Wood said. "Me, I prefer to go by Murphy's Law and be ready for when things go wrong."

"Fair enough," Molvico said. "Think we should give it a try tonight?"

Wood shook her head. "No sense rushing. I say we take time to line things up and make our move tomorrow night."

"I hear you," Molvico said. With a grin, he added, "I gotta say, though, I was getting a little horny thinking about it."

"You're sick."

"Just human." Molvico eyed Wood seductively. "Say, how about if when we get back to the room we give Sam the night off and—"

"In your dreams, hotshot," Wood interrupted. "Sorry, I don't mix pleasure with my business."

6

Jotuwi Port, Malaysia

"I think you're onto something," Mack Bolan told Barbara Price, speaking on a secure phone line linking him with the mission controller at Stony Man Farm. "I'll run with it."

"Good. Akira is putting together a file with Satcam photos," Price told him. "Do you have access to your laptop?"

"It'll take me a minute to track it down, but yeah," Bolan responded.

"I'll send it to you, then, along with the mug shots and anything else we've come up with on our end."

"Sounds like a plan."

"I hope it pans out," Price said. "And once the dust settles, if you want to detour up to Hong Kong and check out this kidnapping business, feel free. Hal says Scott Kelmin's been making calls to the President asking for a little extra help anyway."

"Given all the money Kelmin kicked into his election campaign, I'm not surprised," Bolan responded.

"If I didn't know any better, I'd say you're being cynical," Price teased.

"I just call them like I see them," Bolan stated. "But, yeah, I'll look into it."

Bolan wrapped up the call, then rejoined Anthony Tetlock. The UN official was standing alongside the Humvee originally intended for use in busting the ill-fated rendezvous back at the end of the dirt road leading from Jotuwi Port. Bolan's computer was stashed away in his gear bag inside a second Humvee parked just inside a cordoned-off area of the harbor's warehouse facilities.

Tetlock had spent the past hour helping tie up loose ends following the brief skirmish in the harbor involving Maritime troops and the Aceh separatists. The Kiowa search choppers had refueled and returned to the jungle, still looking for triad ringleader Jiang Yang.

After his conversation with Barbara Price, however, Bolan had a feeling there might be a better place to find their man. "There's a salvage yard a mile north of here," Bolan told Tetlock, passing along the information Price, in turn, had received from Akira Tokaido. "I have it on good authority that the place is run by a San Hop Kwan outfit from Kuala Lumpur. If Yang made it out of the jungle, he might have gone there."

"I know the place," Tetlock said. "Let me put something together and we'll check it out."

"I've got some satellite images coming in for us to work from," Bolan said, reaching into the nearest Humvee for his gear bag.

"That would be helpful." Tetlock narrowed his eyes and regarded Bolan thoughtfully. "You must be pretty well connected to be able to snap your fingers and come up with something like that so quick."

"I manage," Bolan replied.

All Tetlock knew about Bolan was the cover story he'd been given when the Executioner had first arrived in Malaysia. Bolan was working under his Matt Cooper alias, with his ID listing him as a special op for the Justice Department. Tetlock had been told that any other background information was classified on a need-to-know basis. Tetlock could fish all he wanted, but curiosity wasn't grounds enough for Bolan to break his cover and both men knew it.

"*Ask me no questions, I'll tell you no lies,* is that it?" Tetlock said with a stiff grin.

"Something like that," Bolan said. "No offense."

"No offense taken," Tetlock said. "If you can help us wrap this up, I don't care if you're secretly from the North Pole."

The UN officer excused himself and grabbed a microphone from the transceiver mounted beneath the dash of his Humvee. As Tetlock patched through a call to the chopper pilots, Bolan crouched over his gear bag and opened it, taking out his notebook computer. As he waited for it to boot up, he paced a few steps back and forth, testing his hamstring. Before changing into some dry clothes he'd sheathed his upper leg with a rubberized sleeve that offered support without unduly hindering his mobility. The hamstring felt sore, but he wasn't about to let it sideline him. Not with a mission at stake.

Thinking back on his conversation with Barbara Price, Bolan felt an increased determination to move on to Hong Kong once he'd tended to Jiang Yang and whatever triad colleagues might still holed up at the salvage yard. The kidnapping of Eva Kelmin had touched a nerve with him, taking him back, years ago, to his native Pittsfield, where his sister had been dragged into prostitution due to their father's involvement with the local Mafia, prompting the disintegration of his family and the beginning of his War Everlasting.

That battle, of course, was a long way from running its course, and the Executioner had found himself back on long-familiar ground, only this time the Mob he was up against traced its origins, not back to the island of Sicily, but rather mainland China. No matter. Their modus operandi remained the same. Just as the Mafia preyed on the weak and defenseless and amassed its power by corrupting the societal order around them, so did the triads. Bolan was determined to go for the jugular of their Chinese counterparts.

7

Hong Kong

Eva Kelmin splashed cold water on her face, then briefly held a washcloth under the running tap water. Once she'd wrung out the cloth, she strode wearily from the bedroom and threw herself on the bed. Her eyes were puffy from crying and she used the cloth as a compress, hoping to reduce the swelling.

One of the first things the eighteen-year-old had learned after being pressed into duty at the Dynasty was that clients were turned off by tears or any display of sadness. And if word got back to the men out front that she'd been weeping, there would be consequences. Meals withheld, privileges denied, and, if one of her captors was in a foul mood, she could expect a beating. And these men—especially Li Chuannan, the resident bouncer—knew how to hurt a woman without leaving bruises, which would be counterproductive to business. Or, worse yet, there would be the shots, painful injections that induced cramps and vomiting. She'd had the shots once, her first day, and she never wanted to go through that experience again. She'd learned quickly that the only way to make her life in this prison tolerable was to play the game, to meet clients with a smile and learn what pleased them, then see to it that they left the room satisfied. The women who played the game well enough were spared the dreariness of the windowless inner rooms. Like Kelmin, the women who played the game got the large suites overlooking the street. And along with it they got the better clients, men less inclined to abuse or perversities. It was like in Dante's *Inferno*, one of the last things she'd read before dropping out of high school. There were different circles of Hell, and the deeper one went into the abyss, the worse things got. Kelmin was determined to stay on the outer circle.

There was a small round speaker imbedded in the ceiling of her room, an intercom allowing the men up front to listen in while she was with clients to make sure she didn't say anything to jeopardize the enterprise. They could talk to her over the intercom as well, and shortly after she heard a telltale crackle over the speaker, Kelmin cringed at the sound of an all-too familiar voice—Hu Dzem, the brothel's hands-on proprietor.

"You have a client," Dzem told her. His English was good but it'd taken Kelmin a few days to understand his pronunciation. "Mandarin. He's on his way up."

"Yes, sir," Kelmin replied obediently. Hu Dzem liked obedience.

"He says he likes fellatio. Bareback."

Kelmin yanked the compress from her eyes and wadded it tightly in her fist, reining in her disgust.

"Did you hear me?"

"Yes, sir," she responded. "I'll see to it that he has a good time."

"That's what we like to hear."

Kelmin glared at the speaker. She hid her hand under the washcloth and gave Hu Dzem the finger. She had to do it discreetly because the other girls had said there were hidden cameras in the rooms allowing the men up front to spy on them as well as eavesdrop. Some even said that tapes were made of their encounters and bootlegged overseas to sex shops in the States and in Europe. The idea appalled her, especially when she considered the idea that someone might recognize her and tell her father.

Eva was Scott Kelmin's only child. The two of them had never gotten along and when their relationship had soured even further after her mother's death, there had been times when she wanted nothing better than to hurt the old man any way she could. Being a juvenile delinquent had been a good first step, angering and frustrating the media mogul to no end. That hadn't been enough, though. She'd wanted to shame him, to tarnish his reputation and make him pay for all the times he'd neglected her in favor of his work. When she'd decided to run away from home, she'd figured that would do the trick. She'd make him sick with worry, make him regret every mean thing he'd ever said or done to her. And within a few days after leaving home, it'd looked like it was working. The messages he'd left on her cell phone were at first hostile, filled with the usual guilt mongering and contempt. When she hadn't responded, the tone had softened, first to impatience and then exasperation. In the last call she'd received, he'd actually sounded contrite and apologetic. *"Please, Evie,"* he'd implored. *"Please call home."*

By then, however, it had been too late. By then she'd fallen in with Jiang Yang and bought into all his talk about modeling opportunities overseas.

All lies.

By the time she realized what a mistake she'd made, Yang had taken her cell phone along with her ID, her passport and all the rest of her belongings. He'd brought her to Hong Kong and turned her over to Hu Dzem. She had doubts that she would ever see her father again. And there were nights when her work was over and she was free to cry herself to sleep that she yearned for nothing so much as the chance to return home and run into her father's arms, tell him how sorry she was for the grief she'd caused him.

There was a knock on the door.

"Coming." Kelmin sat up on the edge of the bed, cursing to herself as she wiped the tears from the corners of her eyes.

She was wearing an ankle-length red satin robe over black lingerie fringed with lace. She stabbed her feet into a pair of high-heeled pumps, then stood and grabbed a perfume atomizer from the nightstand. As she spritzed herself, she glanced out toward the street. The shades drawn across the sliding glass door leading to the balcony were sheer enough that she could make out twinkling lights in the branches of the acacias that lined the median strip along Hennessey Avenue. There was something reassuring about the view, however obscured, just as she found comfort in the sound of traffic and the occasional shouts of pedestrians on the sidewalk below. It was a reminder that there was another way of life out there, just beyond this outer circle of hell. Somehow it gave her hope.

The man in the hallway was about to knock again when Kelmin opened the door, smiling brightly.

"Come in," she cooed in Mandarin. It was one of several phrases she'd been taught since arriving in Hong Kong. *Come in. You are very handsome. What a man you are. Do you like it when I do this? Please come back again.* It amazed her how little had to be said to get through a session and leave a man smiling.

Kelmin's client was middle-aged, perhaps a few years older than her father. He had thinning hair, bland features and small eyes magnified by a pair of horn-rimmed glasses. She smelled liquor on his breath as she took his hand and led him into the room and closed the door. His palm was sweating and she could feel him shaking. She guided him across the room and then sat down on the edge of the bed. Looking up at him, she continued to smile, fingering loose the sash around her waist. Slowly she parted the robe, revealing her low-cut brassiere and the faint swell of her breasts. Reaching for the man's waist, Eva began to unfasten the his belt. Whispering seductively, she told him, "You are very handsome…."

Hu Dzem could trace his lineage back four centuries to the origins of the triads, when secret societies first sprang. Legend had it that Dzem's ancestors had been struggling farmers in the northern Chinese provinces before throwing in their lot with outlaw factions. His forefathers had proved more adept at crime than agriculture, and many a generation had passed since anyone in the family tree had soiled his hands working the fields.

Hu Dzem was no exception. By the time he was ten, he'd dropped out of school to run numbers for an uncle, and when he'd reached manhood he was elevated to the status of Dai Lo, or Big Brother, and given his own slice of territory to run. He'd done his job well, slowly building power through alliances with other ringleaders.

Two years earlier there had been a power void in the upper ranks following the unexpected death of San Hop Kwan's chairman. Hu Dzem, by then the group's treasurer, had made his move, seizing control of the organization and its loose-knit network of four thousand members. He ran things from his penthouse suite at the Dynasty, his prized holding, and focused primarily on the traditional vice rackets that had come to be the trademark of San Hop Kwan: loan-sharking, prostitution, drugs and gambling.

Unlike godfathers who governed the American syndicates with dictatorial authority, triad overlords like Dzem held less sway over their underlings. Dai Los had greater autonomy over their operations than capo chiefs in the U.S., and if certain ringleaders chose to branch out into other criminal enterprises than those favored by Dzem, it was considered their right.

Dzem didn't care for the arrangement. In fact, the chairman's feeling was that by spreading their focus into too many areas beyond the time-honored domain, the triads would ultimately dilute their power and influence. He, for one, had long cautioned against the black-market brokering of arms, especially those with nuclear capabilities, feeling the such activities made the triad vulnerable to too many external law-enforcement agencies.

This night, much to his chagrin, Hu Dzem had just learned that his warnings had not only gone unheeded, but had resulted in a situation he felt certain would bring down heat on the organization. The word from his sources in Malaysia was that things had gone awry with a nuclear centrifuge transaction involving Jiang Yang—one of his more wayward Dai Los—and rebel insurgents from the Indonesian province of Aceh.

The affair had all the markings of an international incident, the kind that invariably led to outside agencies shining a light on the activities of San Hop Kwan. With the triad mere weeks away from holding its annual election for office leaders, the development would likely have far-reaching repercussions.

Perhaps, he thought, in the wake of the incident he would gain votes from those who sided with his views about nontraditional enterprises, but the chairman also realized there would be those who looked at the situation with a more jaundiced eye and would wonder why Dzem had allowed such a foolhardy transaction to be attempted in the first place. If he was perceived as too weak to control those within his innermost circle, there might well rise a cry through the ranks that he'd gone too soft to effectively hold dominion, however honorary, over the whole organization. He knew already that there was growing clamor in the ranks for fresh blood at the top. This recent development could easily swell the dissent, making him vulnerable to defeat in the election. Such a disgrace, Hu Dzem felt, would be the ruin of him.

"I told them!" Dzem railed as he slammed down the phone in his penthouse office. "I told them it would come to this!"

He pushed himself away from the desk and rose from his chair. Fifty years old, Dzem was a short, stocky man with shock-white hair combed straight back from his pronounced forehead. He had a weakness for tanning lotions, which had left his skin with a dark cast that was less bronze than the color of an overbaked pumpkin. His fashion tastes were equally ill-advised, as he favored tight-fitting sharkskin suits that exaggerated his girth, and wore an array of gold jewelry far more gaudy than impressive. More than one news reporter had pointed out that Dzem looked like a walking parody straight out of a bad Hollywood movie.

The chairman continued to rant as he made his way past two solemn-faced bodyguards to a wet bar near the wide picture window facing north, past the rooftops of the sleaze joints on Lockhart Avenue to the moonlit waters of Victoria Harbour.

Besides Hu Dzem and his bodyguards, the only other person in the room was the bouncer Li Chuannan. Chuannan pretended to ignore the brothel owner's outburst and averted his gaze to the bank of monitors linked to various surveillance cameras mounted throughout the brothel.

One of the screens showed Eva Kelmin and her Mandarin client. Chuannan was expressionless as he watched the sexual transaction. It was nothing he hadn't seen a hundred times before. His mind was elsewhere. The news from Malaysia impacted on Chuannan in more ways than Hu Dzem knew, and the enforcer sensed that his life was on the verge of change, a change almost as dramatic as the one that had led to his current employment.

Less than three years earlier, Li Chuannan had been a professional wrestler, playing heel in the ring under the stage name Juggernaut. He looked the part, standing six-three with his already ample physique filled out even further by regular steroid injections. The steroids had given him bad skin and a surly disposition that had made him an easy magnet for crowd jeers. His manager had told him it was a good thing for him to be booed, but Chuannan had been unable to grasp the concept and had instead taken the jeers personally. At first he'd vented his anger on his ring opponents and for a few months he'd been wildly successful, holding down the heavyweight belt while starring regularly at the top of the card for the Pac-Rim Wrestling promotion. His reputation was such that he'd eventually received an offer to make the big jump to U.S. Championship Wrestling.

By then, however, his steroid rage had gotten out of hand. In addition to throttling opponents in the ring, he'd begun to tear apart locker rooms and go into the stands to confront American fans taunting him by his new name, Ri-Zing Sung. The crowd had fed on what they thought was merely a loose cannon gimmick and soon he was greeted at every venue by chants of "Sung Sucks! Sung Sucks!" Two weeks into his first road trip through the Deep South, Chuannan had snapped, pile-driving a particularly obnoxious Fort Lauderdale fan headfirst onto the concrete floor of the local armory.

Paralyzed, the fan had filed a twenty million dollar lawsuit against Chuannan and USCW. The case had been settled out of court, but by then Chuannan had been sent back to China. His reputation had followed him and he'd been treated like a pariah on the Asian wrestling circuit.

The triads, however, always had a use for dim-witted goons with an appetite for violence, and soon Chuannan had found himself part of Hu Dzem's entourage. When he wasn't pulling bouncer duty at the Dynasty, the behemoth could be counted on to provide muscle for Dzem's network of extortionists and loan sharks. So far he'd sent more than a dozen slow-paying clients to the hospital. Another eight had wound up in the morgue. Chuannan didn't mind the work, but he had it in his head that he was meant for better things.

Although he was on good terms with Dzem, Chuannan had a far closer relationship with Jiang Yang. The two had become friends during the time they worked together at the brothel—before Yang had moved on at Dzem's behest once the chairman had learned that the authorities were seeking the Dai Lo in connection with the kidnapping of Eva Kelmin. After hours, Chuannan and Yang had often hit the bars together, and whenever Yang had drinks in him and started talking about the grand plans he had in mind for himself, he'd always made a point to tell Chuannan he could be a part of those plans if he wanted.

"You don't have to spend the rest of your life being Dzem's trained ape," Yang had told him time and again. If it were up to him, Yang always insisted, Chuannan would become a Dai Lo as well. Chuannan liked the sound of that.

Li Chuannan and the bodyguards traded a few smirks behind Hu Dzem's back as they waited for the chairman to finish his venting. They were all used to Dzem's tirades. Once the chairman fell silent and had gotten some more liquor into him, the bouncer finally spoke.

As casually as possible, he asked Dzem, "What happened to Jiang Yang? Was he captured?"

"No," Dzem grumbled, pouring himself another drink. "He wasn't killed, either. No such luck. Why do you ask?"

Li Chuannan shrugged noncommittally. "Just curious."

"Well, he's alive. For now." The chairman drained his tumbler, then wiped his lips with the back of his hand and leveled his gaze at Chuannan. "If he makes it back here, though, we'll have to do something about that—"

8

Jotuwi Port, Malaysia

In the wake of the deadly 2005 tsunami that sent the Indian Ocean raging through coastal communities from Sumatra to Sri Lanka, Jotuwi native Lee-Kuan Mahr had seen opportunity and tried to make the most of it. The owner of a small-scale salvage yard located next to a sluggish, mosquito-infested lagoon stretching from Jotuwi Port to the nearby regional airport, Mahr was among the first to volunteer a place where cleanup crews could unload the countless thousands of tons of debris and rubble excavated from the ruins that had once been seaside resorts and fishing villages.

When the government contracts began to pile up as fast as the heaps of displaced waste arriving daily aboard overloaded garbage scows, Mahr quickly realized he'd bitten off more than he could chew. For assistance, he'd turned to a cousin who was a Dai Lo for a San Hop Kwan affiliate operating out of Kuala Lumpur. To secure the aid of the triad, Mahr had been forced to divulge the master plan behind his seemingly altruistic gesture. Mahr had explained that once trash was hauled to his land, he would have work crews scour the debris for valuables, then evenly disperse the remains across the lagoon. Once the growing haul displaced the lagoon, he would hire out dredges to bring in loads of silt to heap over the deposited garbage. After the makeshift landfill had been compacted and leveled, Mahr would suddenly be in possession of more than fourteen square miles of prime real estate ripe for development.

A scrawled blueprint on a cocktail napkin, complete with envisioned luxury apartments, office complexes and a seaside resort, had been sufficient to draw interest from the crime syndicate. A deal had been struck in which Mahr, somewhat reluctantly, had signed over his deed to the land for a million dollars plus a cut of future profits as well as a guaranteed say in the development process.

Work had begun almost immediately after the pact was agreed to, but the logistics had proved daunting. The triad, used to a more immediate return on its investments, gradually lost interest in the project. Inside of a year, things were moving at a snail's pace. By then, Mahr had also gambled away most of what he'd first assumed would be enough money to last a lifetime. Distraught over his foolishness and impatient with the lack of progress on the landfill, he'd accused the triad of not holding up its end of the agreement and asked to have the property turned over to him so that he could seek out another partner. His argument had fallen on deaf ears. Mahr had become belligerent and even went so far as to say he'd alert the authorities of the triad's involvement if it didn't throw more resources into the project. It was the worst in a long string of bad decisions.

Two days after his threat, Mahr received a late-night visit from a pair of triad goons armed with knives the size of meat cleavers. His left hand was hacked off and he'd have bled to death if one of his workers hadn't heard his cries for help.

Mahr lost the entire forearm and, while recuperating at the hospital, received a visit from his cousin, who passed along word from his superiors that the next time Mahr threatened the triad he would be sliced up again, this time more thoroughly.

Some eight months later, Lee-Kuan Mahr's would-be dream had been reduced to a living nightmare. He lived in a ramshackle mobile home resting on a strip of compacted land between the original salvage yard and the lagoon. It had become clotted with uneven, rank-smelling mounds of trash overrun by flies, rats and other vermin that carried enough disease to insure a state of near-constant ill health to an ever-ready supply of displaced tsunami victims and other hard luck cases desperate enough to join Mahr's workforce in exchange for two meals of steamed rice a day and whatever free lodging they could piece together from the refuse they spent their days combing through.

Any valuables scavenged from the waste heaps were turned over to a band of San Hop Kwan heavies who showed up at the end of each work day and strip-searched everyone to make sure that nothing of worth was held back. The goons also made regular stops at a large Quonset hut erected in the middle of the salvage yard. Workers deemed trustworthy spent their days there helping a crew of San Hop Kwan functionaries manufacture methamphetamines and process heroin smuggled in from the Golden Triangle aboard the same scows hauling debris from places as far away as Phucket Bay and the Burmese Coast.

Occasionally, young girls kidnapped from backcountry villages in Myanmar or Thailand would be kept for a few days at the site, allowing both workers and triad goons a chance for some "recreation" before the girls were shuttled up the coast for a life of forced prostitution at Hu Dzem's string of Hong Kong brothels.

Mahr had given up any hope of ever seeing the landfill project completed, much less the development of resorts or condominiums. In fact, he'd pretty much given up on everything altogether and become content to waste his days holed away in the mildewed living room of his trailer, numbed by painkillers and lost in a haze of opium smoke. He figured the narcotics would kill him eventually, and as far as he was concerned, the sooner it happened the better. He'd had enough of life, which had borne out, all too well, a warning his mother had given at him a lifetime ago. "Make a deal with the devil," she'd told him whenever he misbehaved, "and you will wind up in hell."

For much of the past week, Mahr's squalid quarters had been taken over by a handful of San Hop Kwan members from Hong Kong. The men had helped themselves to Mahr's food and drink, used his VCR to play porno films at night and saw to it that they were among the first to scrounge through the sifted leavings brought to the salvage yard by Mahr's downtrodden workforce. Mahr was none too happy with the arrangement but knew there was little he could do about it.

Earlier this particular day, during a lucid moment between opium fixes, Mahr had heard several of the men talking about borrowing one of the hydrofoils normally used out on the lagoon to help direct the placement of trash. The men had said they wanted to take the craft up one of the tributaries leading into the jungle and made mention of throwing some kind of "surprise party." Mahr had suspected foul play was involved, and as such he'd known it was in his best interests to pretend he hadn't heard anything.

Late into the night, Mahr was roused from his stupor by a yelping from the dozen or more guard dogs patrolling the fenced-off area that encircled his home and the large Quonset hut. Someone shouted for the dogs to shut up, then Mahr heard the creaking hinges of a large gate swinging. He was rubbing drool from his unshaved chin when headlights flashed through the front blinds and a car came to a stop outside. Moments later, one of the triad members—the one with the frighteningly skull-like face—strode inside, peeling a wet shirt from his back. Even with his senses dulled, Mahr could smell the stench clinging to Jiang Yang; it was more foul and stomach turning than the reek of the lagoon.

"What are you looking at?" Yang shouted at Mahr as he kicked off his shoes and began to peel off the rest of his clothes.

Mahr glanced away, turning his attention to the television. The station he'd been watching had gone off the air, and there was nothing on the screen but a test pattern. Given the amount of opium still in his system, Mahr became mesmerized by the pattern. Over the faint buzz of white noise emanating from the set, he heard Jiang Yang toss his clothes outside the front door before heading to the bathroom. The triad ringleader left the door open as he turned on the shower, and soon steam began to spill out into the hallway. Mahr continued to stare at the TV screen, transfixed. As the steam began to curl around his lounge chair and drift toward the television set, the one-armed man again had the sensation that he'd drifted back into his dreams. At the same time, he had another feeling that was even more pronounced. A sudden chill ran through him and he began to tremble in his chair, overcome by an inexplicable sense of dread. It was the same feeling he'd had the night when the triad had sent men to cut off his arm. A premonition.

"Something bad," he murmured to himself helplessly, "is about to happen."

9

Stony Man Farm, Virginia

Akira Tokaido leaned away from his keyboard and called out to Hal Brognola and Barbara Price. "Done. Striker's up to date on everything we could pull together."

"Good," Brognola murmured absently. He and Price were standing before the bank of computer screens lining the far wall, eyes focused on the one depicting a world map highlighted with various hot spots, areas where the Farm's tactical teams were either on assignment or likely to wind up in the near future.

In the United States, a crimson speck flagged the Texas Panhandle, where Able Team—a three-man squad made up of Carl Lyons, Rosario Blancanales and Hermann Schwarz—were in the process of neutralizing a private militia group harboring delusions they could single-handedly bring down the American government by blowing up a convention center where three liberal senators were addressing a civil rights rally. Far across the globe, a winking red dot on the southernmost tip of Malaysia indicated Bolan's position at Jotuwi Port. As for Phoenix Force, the Farm's primary overseas commando force, the unit was still across the straits from Bolan in Aceh, but they wouldn't be there much longer.

Phoenix Force Leader David McCarter had checked, saying he'd just received confirmation that the Aceh separatists being held in Jotuwi Port after the foiled centrifuge transaction were also behind the car-bombing they had been investigating.

Their mission had, in effect, been preempted. The question Brognola faced was where next to send McCarter's crew, not to mention the two additional Stony Man personnel—veteran pilot Jack Grimaldi and weaponsmith John "Cowboy" Kissinger—who'd been working alongside them in Aceh.

"No shortage of options, unfortunately," Brognola said, counting seven orange dots on the map indicating high-priority incidents taking place within a five hundred mile radius of Aceh. "I guess the obvious choice would be to send them to Malaysia so they can team up with Striker."

"Normally I'd agree with you," Price replied, glancing over a printout giving quick rundowns of what was happening in the orange-lit areas, "but things are already in motion there, and I think Phoenix Force might be put to better use over in Bali. There's a hostage situation that just came up involving some Jesuit missionaries from the States. The clock's ticking."

Brognola took the document and quickly read it. Price was right; the Balinese quandary had top priority written all over it. He eyed the mission controller and asked, "What's the fastest set of wings Phoenix can get their hands on?"

"I'd have to check to make sure," Price said, "but I think they have a Navy Prowler at their disposal."

"That'd get them there quick, all right," Brognola replied, "but there's no way you're going to shoehorn seven guys into that thing. Five would be pushing it."

"They could split up," Price suggested. "David could fly three guys out in the Prowler, while Jack takes the rest in something smaller."

Even as he was starting to nod his approval, Brognola felt a stirring in his gut. He'd had the feeling before, and it had less to do with the pangs of a recurring ulcer than something inside him that felt compelled to question obvious choices. He decided to go with his instincts.

"Let's do this," he said. "Send Phoenix to Bali in the Prowler, just like you suggested. As for Jack and Cowboy, I think I'd rather see them split off and head north to Jotuwi."

"Are you sure?" Price said. "The fireworks are likely to be over before they get there."

"Maybe so," Brognola conceded, "but Phoenix can handle things in Bali, and if Striker decides he wants to move on to Hong Kong once he's done there, a little extra manpower might help."

Price held Brognola in her studied gaze. "There's something you're not telling me," she said, guessing.

"What are you talking about?" Brognola protested.

"You're playing one of your hunches, aren't you?" Price said. "You think Striker might run into problems."

Brognola was silent a moment. Finally he said, "Let's just go with my plan, all right?"

Price regarded Brognola, then nodded. "I'll get on it."

As she started off, Price—like Lee-Kuan Mahr and Hal Brognola—felt herself beset by a vague uneasiness.

Something wasn't right....

Jotuwi Port, Malaysia

Bolan pointed to the LCD screen of his notebook computer. "Obviously this is the area we want to concern ourselves with."

He and Anthony Tetlock were staring at a grainy, satellite view of Lee-Kuan Mahr's ill-fated landholding. It was the most recent scan sent to Bolan by Akira Tokaido, taken less than fifteen minutes earlier by an Orion spy satellite diverted from its customary orbital prowl over the Indian Ocean. Bolan had zoomed in on the area of the salvage yard, including the mobile home and Quonset hut, and though some clarity had been sacrificed, the close-up contained enough detail for them to have a good idea what they were looking at.

"This inner perimeter fence is a lot more fortified than the one around the rest of the property," Bolan said.

"Not only that," Tetlock replied, leaning close to the screen for a better look, "but they've got guard dogs around the inner sanctum, if you want to call it that."

The two men were huddled in the rear of Tetlock's Humvee, which had pulled off the main road a hundred yards shy of the main entrance to the salvage grounds. Besides the driver, there were two other commandos in the vehicle. A second vehicle had driven past the entrance, and Bolan knew it would have turned off onto a dirt road running through a vacant parcel of land separating the lagoon from the outermost runway of the Jotuwi Regional Airport. Five of Tetlock's men soldiers were in the other vehicle, awaiting orders on how best to cross onto the salvage property and assist in the apprehension of Jiang Yang.

Bolan had already matched up the overhead view of Yang's getaway vehicle with a series of other Satcam images of a Toyota Tercel making its way from the Malaysian National Rubber Plant to the coast an hour after the ambush that had slain Chief Customs Officer Dato Jamal. That the Tercel was now parked in front of the hut inside the salvage grounds made it a lock, at least in Bolan's mind, that Yang had used the car to elude the Kiowa choppers that had been searching the jungle for him. As for the Kiowas, one had been diverted to harbor patrol while the other two were idling near a freight yard at the airport, awaiting Tetlock's orders. Tetlock didn't want to use the choppers until the last minute, lest they tip off Yang and any cohorts holed up with him at the facility.

Bolan slowly widened the Satcam image on his computer and began to focus on the outermost reaches of the salvage operation. There was something almost surreal about the wide sprawl of land and its heaped mounds of debris. Most of the trash was nondescript, much like that found at any landfill. But here and there larger objects poked out from the rubble: mangled trucks, partially intact walls, and large crumpled signs and billboards. On one strip of land near the lagoon, a handful of people could be seen standing around small campfires set near the overturned hulls of several large ships that had most likely been flung ashore like toys by the force of the tsunami. There were also the fractured shells of smaller yachts and houseboats that, while no longer seaworthy, still provided shelter from the elements.

"Workers compound," Bolan said, recalling data from one of the files Tokaido had e-mailed with the Satcam images.

"Shantytown is more like it," Tetlock replied. "If we can't

nail these bastards for anything else, I'm sure we can throw the book at them for unsafe working conditions."

"Probably," Bolan said. "But we want these guys to get more than a slap on the wrist."

"I won't argue that," Tetlock responded. "One thing I can tell you about these workers, though—they aren't likely to have any sort of allegiance to the people running this hellhole. Once the shit hits the fan, I doubt we'll have to worry about them coming to the aid of the guys we're after."

"I just hope they stay out of the line of fire and let us do what we have to," Bolan said. "It's going to be tricky enough without having to worry about collateral damage."

"What about here?" Tetlock pointed out a spit of land elbowing around the south flank of the lagoon. "The trash is piled high enough for us to reach the inside fence without being seen, and there's some kind of path winding through most of the crap so we wouldn't have to make a lot of racket."

Bolan zoomed in on the image. Tetlock was right. Once they were on the property, it appeared they could use the cranes and a few mounds of debris for additional cover as they closed in on the trailer and Quonset hut.

"I can see some water we'll have to slog through," the Executioner said, "but it shouldn't be that deep."

"Agreed," Tetlock said. "We can have the other crew come in from the other direction using this truck yard for cover."

Bolan nodded, shifting his attention to an area of the Satcam image north of the target zone. The land was crowded with a few dozen large vehicles that looked as if they'd been run through a gigantic pretzel machine. Most of the hoods were propped open, and the engine compartments had been gutted for salvageable parts. As with the approach Bolan and Tetlock had blocked out for themselves, the other team would have to navigate its way through tendrils of brackish water seeping inland from the lagoon.

"One thing in our favor," Tetlock said, "is that security

looks pretty lax. Outside of the dogs and the fence, I see only one guy standing guard duty."

He pointed to a lone figure standing on a walkway that surrounded a two-story water tower situated between the Quonset hut and the trailer. It looked as if the sentry was armed with some kind of assault rifle.

"Let's hope he's flying solo," Bolan said. "But remember these images are from nearly a half hour ago. We might walk into a whole different situation."

"Granted," Tetlock said. "And I suppose there's always the chance they have guys posted out of view around some of these junk heaps."

Bolan nodded, his focus now on a pair of small trucks parked next to each other on the hard-packed dirt surrounding the hut. "Those trucks look like they're in working order, so we have to assume there's more of the enemy out there somewhere. Armed, too, most likely."

"We'll just have to go in with our eyes open," Tetlock said. "I'd like to take those dogs out of the equation somehow, too."

"I've been thinking the same thing," Bolan said, "and I've got an idea that might work."

11

Once he'd showered and changed, Jiang Yang raided Lee-Kuan Mahr's kitchen for something to eat. There wasn't much to choose from, and he had to settle for a few curds of tofu and a bacon-sized strip of jerky washed down with the last few drops left in a ceramic bottle of chilled sake. The concoction did little to satisfy Yang's hunger or improve his mood. He was half tempted to take out his anger on Mahr, but the one-armed man was passed out in his chair, this time for real, and seemed too pathetic a target to bother with. Instead, Yang snatched up the TV remote from the floor where Mahr had dropped it, then flipped through stations until he found a news channel. He busied himself lighting a cigarette, ignoring a story about plans for Chinese New Year Festivities in Kuala Lumpur. He blew smoke on his fingers, hoping to rid them of the lingering stench from the waste pipe he'd clung to at the jungle rubber plant. Both hands were still sore from that ordeal, and he was beginning to notice a faint throbbing in his right shoulder. He began massaging the ache with his left hand, then suddenly stopped.

A news anchor was reporting on the incident in the harbor where UN troops seized a pirated Indonesian freighter after an exchange of gunfire with hijackers. There was no mention the centrifuges, but in a cutaway shot, port officials were shown standing alongside the bundled currency found on the Aceh separatists who'd been taken into custody.

Yang cursed at the sight of the money, money he'd been counting on to bankroll plans to distance himself from the influence of Hu Dzem. He realized it was the chairman who would be having the last laugh. Hu Dzem had told Yang all along that peddling nuclear contraband on the black market was a mistake, and here was all proof the chairman needed to back up his claim.

Yang knew he still had a trump card up his sleeve, an ally who'd allow him to do business without having to answer to the bloated old man with the bad tan. But Yang wasn't ready to play that card yet. For now, like it or not, he still had to deal with Dzem.

Yang was surprised when the news segment ended with no mention of the ambush of Dato Jamal or the fact that the triad was in any way connected to either incident. It made no sense to him.

Surely the authorities had implicated San Hop Kwan, he thought. The fact that they were withholding information didn't bode well. Yang had been counting on them tipping their hand so he might better judge how to deal with matters. Now, he would have to proceed with even more caution. That or ask his counterparts from Kuala Lumpur if they had any moles within local enforcement. He didn't want to go that route, either. He hated the KL crew, especially their Dai Lo, Rhy Vhal, a ferret-eyed whelp three years younger than Yang with an ego the size the Forbidden City. No way was he going to wind up owing that bastard any favors.

Lee-Kuan Mahr stirred in his chair and began to snore. Yang scowled at the landowner, then snapped off the television and dropped the remote back on the floor. He went back to his room long enough to grab a 9 mm Glock and tuck it inside the waistband of his clean pants. Eager to get away from the salvage yard as soon as possible, Yang spit at Mahr as a form of farewell, then made his way from the trailer. Outside, a trio of guard dogs was chasing one another around the Tercel, but the pack stopped its game at the sight of Yang and began to growl.

"Try it," Yang threatened them, reaching for his Glock. "I know some good restaurants looking for cheap dog meat."

The dogs continued to growl but made no move toward Yang. He circled past them and rounded the parked trucks, glancing up at the sentry posted on the railed walkway surrounding the watertower. The guard had had his Dragunov sniper rifle aimed at one of the dogs. "I've been waiting for an excuse to shut those things up for good," the sentry said, raising his rifle. "How did things go with you?"

"You saw me come back alone," Yang snapped back. "How do you think it went?"

The sentry fell silent. Yang glared at him a moment longer, then headed into the Quonset hut. Inside, cigarette smoke clouded the bank of sputtering fluorescent lights suspended from the high, curved ceiling of the cavernous enclosure. The hut was bustling with activity. To Yang's immediate right, two armed San Hop Kwan enforcers from Kuala Lumpur were helping four workers box a week's worth of processed heroin and crystal meth.

Yang figured the drug shipment would bring in a few million dollars, but none of it would reach his pockets because the operation was run by Rhy Vhal, as was the brokering of any goods scavenged from the waste heaps. That enterprise took up much of the rest of the Quonset hut, making use of a mazelike combination of workbenches, stock shelves and loading docks. Another dozen men were sorting the day's take and transferring goods from the benches to the shelves, which were meticulously organized. The lower shelves were reserved for heavy items such as auto parts and furniture, while jewelry, watches and other small plunder was placed up higher.

In the far corner of the hut, a third group of gangsters sat pouring over stacks of correspondence and pieces of personal identification scavenged from the trash. Surprisingly, this had turned out to be the most lucrative phase of the entire salvage operation. Rhy Vhal had bragged to Yang that identity theft was bringing in a greater cash flow than all of the site's other ventures combined. Yang had boasted back that he would net more from his one nuke transaction than the KL mob was making by, as he'd put it, "scrounging through other people's garbage."

Vhal was working at one of the far tables, wearing a leather vest that allowed him to display the other tattoos he'd had needled into his flesh along with the emblematic San Hop Kwan dragon. When he spotted Yang he sauntered over, arms dangling loose at his sides, a sneer on his acne-scarred face. He'd obviously heard the news.

"So, Skull Face," Vhal taunted, "I guess it's true what the Americans like to say about not counting your chickens before they hatch."

Yang stared hard at Vhal.

"What, no more boasting?" Vhal laughed. "No waving money in our faces and mocking our humble garbage scrounging?"

Yang's arms began to tense. "I'm here to get my men and leave," he responded coolly, gesturing at the two surviving men he'd brought with him from Hong Kong. The men were seated at a nearby table, playing cards with several KL hardmen who were wagering bits of reclaimed jewelry instead of poker chips.

"That's what I figured when I saw you come in with your tail between your legs." Vhal had deliberately raised his voice so his colleagues could overhear. There were a few snickers among those loading the drug shipment.

"Easy for you to talk big with twenty of your men against three of us," Yang responded, letting his right hand trail to his side within easy grasp of his fighting chain.

Vhal smirked at his men, then turned back to Yang. "If

you'd like, we can step outside and discuss things man-to-man."

All work had ceased inside the hut. All eyes were on Yang and Vhal. Yang kept his gaze trained on Vhal, but out of the corner of his eyes he could see hands moving toward holstered pistols and any other weapon within easy reach. He knew he had nothing to gain and everything to lose by provoking matters any further. "I'm here to get my men and leave," he repeated.

"I see," Vhal responded. "I have no problem with that. There is one thing, though. One small thing before you go."

Yang's cohorts rose and moved from the poker table. When one of them let his hand drift too close to the handgun tucked inside his pants, he suddenly found four larger weapons aimed at him, including a sawed-off Remington shotgun. The man froze.

"You disrespected us earlier," Vhal told Yang. "Offer us an apology, then you can go wherever you wish."

"Move against us and you'll have to answer to Hu Dzem," Yang warned, skirting the truth. "We're here under his orders."

"That's not much of an apology," Vhal responded. "And as for answering to the honorable chairman, we'll take our chances. We both know you're far from being one of his favorite sons."

His bluff called, Yang knew he was out of options. He had to back down or face a rout that would likely leave him and his men dead. His choice seemed clear, but Yang's pride wouldn't let him kowtow to the other man. Not under these circumstances. Yang had known from the moment he joined the triad that one day he would likely die at the hand of violence. If this had to be that day, so be it.

Resigned to his fate, the gangster hesitated a moment, deciding whether to go for his fighting chain or the Glock. In that one moment, everything changed, as the charged silence was broken by the sound of an explosion outside the compound.

12

Anthony Tetlock lowered his M-16 and peered through the brush growing up around the rusting cast-iron stove he and another member of his team were crouched behind. The men had cut their way through the outer fence separating the salvage yard from the main road and advanced twenty yards inside the compound. The inner fence was another thirty yards ahead. Tetlock gazed at the hole he'd just put in it with the carbine's sub-mounted M-203 grenade launcher. As he'd hoped, the dogs had been drawn by the explosion and were now rushing through the opening. A deep, trash-filled gully lay between the dogs and the men and Tetlock doubted the beasts would bother testing the obstacle course.

As Tetlock reached to his side for a bowling-pin-sized flame grenade, the other man, retired SAS Lieutenant. Bryce O'Shayne, aimed his bipod-mounted Patriot Arms Genesis sniper rifle at the water tower. Once the enemy sentry had scrambled into view on the tower walkway to check on the disturbance, O'Shayne placed the man in the crosshairs of his scope and pulled the trigger. The Genesis bucked sharply into his shoulder as a 7.62 mm NATO round surged through the twenty-inch barrel. Seconds later, the sentry dropped his assault rifle and toppled over the railing to the ground.

By then Tetlock's flame grenade was airborne, tumbling end-over-end through the night air. The projectile hit the ground and exploded three yards from the makeshift opening in the fence, releasing a fireball into the surrounding brush. Smoke plumed up as the flames spread, creating an instant firewall guaranteed to keep the dogs from returning to the inner compound.

"Worked like a charm," Tetlock murmured.

"Yeah, but we've got a new problem on our hands now," O'Shayne replied, shifting the rifle on its bipod mount.

Tetlock tracked the other man's aim. Through the growing cloud of smoke, the UN official saw a stream of armed gunmen charge out of the Quonset hut.

"New problem is right," Tetlock confirmed.

THE CONFRONTATION between Jiang Yang and Rhy Vhal ended the moment both men heard a rifle shot follow the initial explosion. The sickly thump of the slain sentry's body striking the dirt outside the hut dismissed any doubts as to what was happening.

"Is this your doing?" Vhal raged at Yang as his men began to rush the doorway.

"Of course not!" Yang countered, reaching for his Glock.

Vhal's gun was already out and he had the drop on Yang, but he held back on the trigger. "We'll settle our differences later."

Yang ignored the threat and turned to his men, signaling for them to join the others. It was clear to him that the authorities had somehow tracked him to the salvage yard. Little did they know that in the process of trying to hunt him down they'd actually spared his life, at least for the time being. Yang was determined to somehow make the best of his reprieve.

When the first men charging out through the main door were met with rifle fire, Vhal called out for the others to try the side exits. The goon squad shifted course, making its way past the table where the drugs were being loaded for shipment. There, the trustees had dropped to the ground and scurried beneath the table, afraid for their lives.

Yang waited until Vhal took his eyes off him, then fell in with the other hardmen, placing himself at the rear of the chaotic formation. As the others bolted through the side doors, Yang hung back, then rolled to the floor. Instead of the loading table, however, he took cover behind a steel shelving unit stocked with engine blocks and other large pieces of salvaged machinery. He'd decided he would let the others tend to the enemy. For now, Yang had only one thing in mind: to escape.

BOLAN AND HIS two-man EID crew were slogging through ankle-deep water flanked by refuse heaps when they heard the firefight begin to escalate. The trash blocked their view, but given the number of gunshots being fired, Bolan guessed the others had run into greater resistance than expected. The plan had been for his team to wend through the labyrinth of debris until they were closer to the inner compound, but the Executioner quickly reassessed and decided on another course.

"Spread out and take higher ground," he called to the others. "We need to see what's going on out there."

Slinging his M-16 carbine over his shoulder, Bolan ventured from the muck and began to scale the nearest trash heap. The slope was unstable and loose debris gave way under his weight, forcing him to claw for handholds to keep from backsliding into the water. Several rats, startled from their lairs inside the heap, scurried into view and bounded past. The Executioner ignored them and continued making his way upward. He stopped briefly when Tetlock's voice crackled over the earbud transceiver linked to the walkie-talkie clipped to his waist.

"They sprang a reception committee on us," Tetlock said.

"So I hear," Bolan whispered gruffly. "How many?"

"Hard to say," Tetlock replied. "They're coming out from all sides of the hut. Fifteen, maybe twenty. We got the sentry and drew the dogs out, but the smoke's working against us now."

"What about the other team?" Bolan asked.

"They're on the grounds but they're under fire, too," Tetlock said. "I've called in the Kiowas, so stay clear of the inner compound. You don't want to be in the line of fire if they start letting loose with their pod rockets."

"Got it." Bolan glanced over his shoulder and saw the other two men making their way up nearby trash mounds. "We're nearly in position to lend some fire," he told Tetlock.

"Good. It'll keep 'em from scattering until the choppers show. Once we get past the smoke we'll do the same."

"Stay clear of those dogs," Bolan warned.

"You, too. I've lost sight of them but they're out there."

Bolan signed off and resumed scaling the unstable mound, dropping to his stomach once he neared the top, ignoring the pokes and jabs from sharp-edged debris. His leg was holding up. A small consolation given the circumstances, he thought.

Lying flat across the makeshift ridgeline, Bolan unslung his M-16 and brought it into firing position. To his dismay, he realized his view was still obstructed by another slag heap. The trailer was hidden and all he could see of the Quonset hut was the curved roof. The water tower was another matter. Bolan could see the reservoir tank as well as the surrounding walkway. Two men had just reached the platform and dropped to a crouch, aiming their assault rifles northward. When they began firing, Bolan knew they'd spotted the third UN team advancing on them.

Bolan's M-16 wasn't designed for sniping, but he wasn't about to lie back and let the other men be picked off. Cradling the stock against his shoulder, he took aim and cut loose, sweep-firing to compensate for the carbine's limited accuracy. He nailed one of the riflemen, dropping him to the walkway gridwork. The second gunman retreated behind the tower, unscathed, then whirled about and sent a storm of jacketed shells Bolan's way.

The first rounds missed, but Bolan knew he'd be a marked

man if he didn't make some kind of move, fast. He didn't want to backtrack and take himself further from the fight, so, after spending the rest of his magazine driving the sniper back, Bolan rolled forward and tumbled down the far side of the trash heap. When he reached level ground, he found himself on a wider path than the one he'd taken after broaching the salvage grounds. Parked next to him was a four-ton forklift with a tall load of dented washers strapped to its prongs. There were deep tracks in the mud leading to and away from the forklift, and the indentations matched the lifter's tire treads, meaning the machine was operable. Bolan climbed into the driver's cab. There were keys in the ignition.

"Score one for the good guys," he said.

13

Jack Grimaldi jockeyed the controls of a Grumman F-14 Tomcat borrowed from the Navy carrier *USS Ronald Reagan* and banked through the cotton candy of a cloud formation, then leveled out at twelve thousand feet. He was flying over the Indian Ocean, close enough that he could make out a few ships heading toward the winking lights of Singapore and the southern tip of the Malaysian peninsula. He checked the time on his instrument panel, then told John Kissinger, "Ten minutes to touchdown."

Kissinger was riding directly behind Grimaldi in the flight officer's seat, radio-imbedded headgear matting down his dark hair.

"Gotcha," Kissinger responded. His eyes were on the weapons systems' heads-up display—HUD. Gunner duty wasn't his forte, but he had a passing familiarity with the controls and had been pressed into service enough times to know the drill. If need be, he felt confident he could hone in on a target and help Grimaldi bring the jet's considerable arsenal into play. However, from the briefing he and Grimaldi had received from Aaron Kurtzman before taking to the air, he was doubtful it would come to that.

"I still think we should've flown backup for Phoenix Force," he said. "Seems a shame to have this flying popgun go to waste on a pickup operation."

"I copy that," Grimaldi said, "but orders are orders. Besides, I think the boys were feeling a little cramped by the extra manpower and... Hold on a sec."

Grimaldi tapped his headset, switching over to a secure-link trans-global call from Aaron Kurtzman at Stony Man headquarters in Virginia. He got in a few words but mostly listened. Once he signed off, he shifted course and passed along the update.

"Change in plans," he told Kissinger. "The Satcams are apparently picking up an all-out brawl at that salvage yard Striker's at. From the sound of it, if we haul ass we might just get a chance to pitch the bottom of the ninth."

Jotuwi Port, Malaysia

WHEN A COLLEAGUE CROUCHED beside Rhy Vhal let out a groan and dropped to the ground, skull pulverized by a shot to the head, the Dai Lo cursed and grabbed the man's fallen rifle, hell-bent on retaliation. The gangster was huddled next to a garbage container behind Lee-Kuan Mahr's trailer, where he'd taken cover after exchanging gunshots with the force that had stolen onto the salvage grounds from the north. Vhal braved a few rounds of incoming fire, scanning the perimeter until muzzle-flashes tipped him off to the enemy's position. Taking aim, he disgorged the last few shots in his magazine. When there was no return fire, he hoped that he'd found his mark. But he knew there were still plenty of other targets to contend with.

Lacking backup ammo for his rifle, Vhal cast the weapon aside in favor of his Browning Hi-Power pistol. He was thumbing off the safety when his flagging spirits took another blow.

On the horizon, the lights of a helicopter blinked into view. Judging from flight path, Vhal guessed the bird was headed his way from the nearby airfield. Worse yet, he could make out the silhouette of a second chopper bringing up the rear. When a harsh shaft of light streaked down from the underbelly of the first Kiowa Warrior, Vhal knew the odds of turning the battle's tide in his favor were dwindling by the second.

Vhal could hear gunfire all around him, but for the moment he was no longer in the direct line of fire. Taking advantage of the lull, the gangster broke cover, racing past the water tower. Two of his men had replaced their fallen colleagues on the walkway and were firing at the enemy.

"Keep at it!" Vhal called up to them.

"They've got choppers coming in!" one of the men shouted.

"I'll deal with that!" Vhal yelled back. "Keep at it!"

Another fallen gunman lay dead in the dirt in front of the nearest doorway to the Quonset hut. Vhal stepped over the body and rushed inside. There, he was greeted by two 9 mm rounds from a Walther P-38. One shot whizzed past his right ear. The other caught him in the side, glancing off a rib before exiting through his back. He felt as if he'd been stabbed but ignored the wound, dropping to his knees and swinging his gun in the direction the shots had been fired from.

His first thought was that Jiang Yang had been lying in wait for him, but he spotted two of the trustees standing next to an oversized cabinet that served as the compound's armory. They'd apparently broken the lock and armed themselves. Vhal could see that one of the men had also stuffed the inside of his shirt with some of the drug parcels he'd earlier been helping to package.

It took Vhal a split second to size up the situation and return fire. He was far better trained with a gun than the trustees and managed to drill both men without taking another hit. One man was dead by the time Vhal caught up with them. The other he finished off with a close-range shot to the head.

"Trustees, my ass," he fumed.

Blood was seeping down Vhal's side. He quickly ripped open his leather vest to inspect the damage. It was a clean in-out flesh wound that would likely cost him a few pints of blood and be slow in healing, but there was no time to deal with it. He tried to block out the pain as he threw open the cabinet doors and reached past the AK-47s and other carbines for a shoulder-mount missile launcher armed with a Stinger warhead. He hadn't foreseen a use for such a weapon when he'd stockpiled the cabinet, but he was glad he had it at his disposal, because even as he was securing a grip on the weapon, the thin corrugated steel walls of the hut began to reverberate from the thundering rotor wash of the first Kiowa Warrior.

THE BRUSHFIRE WAS STILL raging, mostly outside the inner compound, and in addition to dry weeds, some of the more flammable trash had ignited, blackening the smoke clouds and giving off an acrid smell. Tetlock's eyes burned as he and O'Shayne tried to circle around the drifting haze. Both men coughed as the foul air tainted their lungs. Finally, they reached a point where they could once again see the hut.

Tetlock scanned the surrounding grounds and counted at least twelve enemy down. He could also detect muzzle-flashes from another three men firing from behind the trucks as well as the stolen Toyota that Yang had used to escape the jungle.

Overhead, the two Kiowa Warriors hovered, each gunship's twin blades displacing smoke as they raked the compound with their searchlights. When they drew fire, the pilots retaliated with their fore-mounted .50-caliber machine guns, upping the death toll.

"There's a sight for sore eyes," O'Shayne said as he propped his bipod mount on a boulder and sought out a target in his rifle scope.

"I second that." Tetlock had reloaded another 40 mm charge into his carbine's grenade launcher, and swiftly assessed the best way to put the weapon to use. Several San Hop Kwan hardmen had just piled into one of the trucks, a dirt-layered Ford F-150 pickup. One man took the wheel while the others piled in back, then resumed firing at the nearest Kiowa. The driver slammed the Ford into reverse and screeched backward, in the process dodging a .50-caliber torrent raining down from the nearest war chopper.

Tetlock readied his launcher. When the truck lurched forward, heading toward the perimeter gate, he aimed slightly ahead of the vehicle, then sent a 40 mm grenade screaming through the night. The projectile was knocked off course slightly as it tore through the fence, but the subsequent explosion gouged the earth just to the right of the truck's path. Shrapnel combined with the blast's concussive force to rattle the truck and take out one of the front tires. The Ford swerved, its front end clipping a raised section of steel pipe with so much force that momentum sent it somersaulting forward. The men in back were thrown clear while the driver bounced off the steering wheel and cracked the windshield with his skull.

"Nice shot," O'Shayne told Tetlock as he used his sniper rifle to finish off one of the men who'd fallen from the truck.

Whatever euphoria the men might have felt at thwarting the enemy getaway was quickly blunted, when Tetlock saw the telltale cloud streak of a Stinger missile heading toward one of the Kiowas. A second later, the aerial gunship was engulfed by a fiery explosion that showered the hut and nearby grounds with large, blazing shards of twisted metal. The warbird's pulverized fuselage dropped with a sickening crash through the roof of Lee-Kuan Mahr's trailer, turning it into a pyre. A scream sounded from within the burning structure. The hell Mahr's mother had warned him about sought him out and claimed him. Searing flames silenced the one-armed opium addict once and for all.

Tetlock was watching the horror unfold when he suddenly felt as if he'd been blindsided by a sledgehammer. A sniper in the water tower had just nailed him in the right shoulder, just above the flak jacket he'd donned before entering the compound. Tetlock staggered backward and fell to the ground, wincing in pain. Seconds later, a followup shot bored into his thigh.

O'Shayne abandoned his rifle and reached out, hoping to drag Tetlock out of the line of fire. The act of chivalry cost him his life, as the sniper's next round caught him at the base of the neck, severing both his spine and carotid artery. O'Shayne slummed across his colleague, showering him with blood.

"Bastards," Tetlock shouted. He tried to move out from underneath the corpse, but he was losing blood fast himself and didn't have the strength. In a matter of seconds, both he and O'Shayne lay still in the brush.

14

The Executioner had driven the forklift clear of the trash heaps when he saw the Kiowa go down. That the enemy was armed with surface-to-air missiles threw a whole new and disturbing wrinkle into things. Still, he saw no other option than to carry out the plan he'd formulated. He figured the closer he could get to the inner compound, the better his chances of seeing to it that the remaining chopper could avoid the same fate as its counterpart.

It was hard for him to see past the forklift's bulky load, which also hindered his already limited maneuverability. To make sure the way before him was clear, Bolan had to lean out of the cab, exposing himself to enemy fire. Doing so, he caught a fresh glimpse of the one of the riflemen posted on the water tower walkway. The sniper had been firing in the direction of the main road, where Bolan assumed Tetlock and O'Shayne were positioned, but once he became aware of the advancing forklift, the rifleman pivoted. The next thing Bolan knew, 7.62 mm rounds were hammering the slow-moving hauler. Bullets clanged off the siding and rattled about the salvage heaped on the front prongs.

Bolan drew his head back inside the cab. He was on a set course, bearing down on the inner perimeter fence. He kept his foot on the gas and one hand on the wheel. In his other hand was his Beretta 93-R, foregrip folded in front of the trigger guard. When a pair of dogs suddenly bounded out from behind a trash heap and started for the forklift, he leveled the pistol and dropped one of the dogs in its tracks with a 3-round burst. The other animal quickly turned heel and fled.

The forklift reached the fence, shearing one of the upright posts and shuddering faintly as it crashed through the barrier. Bolan wrestled the steering wheel, veering the hauler's course toward the water tower. Several flaming bits of the downed chopper were crushed under the lift's tires as it rolled forward. Bolan could hear more enemy rounds bash into the vehicle's thick metal hide and knew the sniper was still firing at him.

There was a toolbox on the bench seat next to Bolan. He slammed his Beretta back in its web holster, then grabbed the box and set it on the floorboard so that its weight replaced his foot on the gas pedal. Bolan waited a second longer to make sure the box would stay in place, then tensed his legs and dived out the side of the vehicle. He hit the ground hard and felt his hamstring flare up on him. He wasn't about to pamper the injury, however, not with the bullets chewing divots out of the dirt around him. He went with his momentum and rolled across the ground until he'd reached the cover of the truck Tetlock had flipped over earlier with his grenade launcher.

Bolan's M-16 was still in the forklift, so he helped himself to an AK-47 lying next to a slain triad member sprawled on the dirt to his right. He was preparing to fire up at his tormentor in the water tower when the structure suddenly tilted sharply forward, undermined by the runaway forklift. Bolan saw the sniper stagger on the walkway, clawing at the rail. The tower was toppling too fast, though, and he was thrown over the side, striking the ground a half second before the reservoir tank crashed down on him. It split open and sent a small river of displaced water racing across the compound. The toolbox had become dislodged during the collision and the forklift stalled, rolling to a stop against the tower upright farthest from Bolan. The vehicle had done its job.

Bolan saw that the remaining Kiowa was still aloft, banking over the lagoon and preparing to sweep back over the compound. He shifted his gaze and scanned the grounds for whoever was using the missile launcher. Before he could spot the gunner, however, he heard a frail, yet desperate voice in his earbud transceiver.

"Get away," Tetlock gasped. "Leave the target area!"

"Are you all right?" Bolan asked, glancing over his shoulder through the smoke and flame between him and Tetlock's position.

"Get away," Tetlock repeated. "There's a jet...."

The UN official's voice trailed off to silence.

Bolan wasn't sure what Tetlock was trying to tell him, but there could be no mistaking the urgency in the man's voice. Bolan decided to heed the man's warning. Clutching the AK-47, the Executioner broke away from the disabled truck and half ran, half limped toward the opening in the fence. There was no gunfire dogging his steps this time, but just as he was charging through the opening, the sky overhead lit up as the second Kiowa Warrior felt the fatal bite of another ground-launched Stinger.

RHY VHAL was beside himself with jubilation. Watching flaming remnants of the downed chopper slam into the earth like so many small comets, he drew the still-warm launcher to his face and kissed the firing tube, oblivious to the fact it was burning his lips. He was equally indifferent to his gunshot wound, which he'd sloppily cleansed and taped while inside the Quonset hut. A small trickle of blood had seeped through the bandage, but Vhal was too giddy to worry over trifles. Two shots, two helicopters. Life was good!

The tattooed Dai Lo knew the battle wasn't won yet, but he'd struck a decisive blow—two blows, to be exact—and, buoyed by a sense of pending victory, he cast aside the missile launcher in favor of his Browning Hi-Power, determined to sustain his side's momentum.

Immediately after bringing down the first Kiowa, Vhal had raced from his position to the cover of a dozen misshapen refrigerators and ice boxes piled haphazardly a dozen yards behind the hut. From there, amid the appliances, the young ringleader had reloaded his launcher and put it to use bringing down the second chopper.

Emboldened by his triumph, he left the cover of the junk heap and stalked brazenly through the firelit grounds. He'd made it as far as the abandoned forklift when he was driven back to cover by shots coming southward from two surviving members of the enemy team. He could see the men in the bonfirelike glow of the second Kiowa, which had slammed to earth just beyond the inner perimeter fence. They were circling around the fence, headed toward the opening created by the forklift.

Vhal propped an elbow on the rear of the forklift and used both hands to steady his aim. He unleashed the rest of his 13-round magazine and grinned as he saw both men go down well short of the opening, one mortally wounded by a head shot, the other dropped by slugs to his right leg and shin.

"This is getting too easy." Vhal laughed.

BOLAN CROUCHED JUST outside the perimeter fence behind another of the salvage cranes, this one equipped with a large electromagnetic lifting tong. He saw two UN men drop, then traced the likely trajectory of the shots that had felled them. Between the smoke and flames from all the scattered fires it was hard for him to spot the shooter. He could barely even discern the outline of the forklift.

Bolan looked back at the downed UN commandos. He could tell one of them was dead. He was about to rush to the other's aid when there was renewed fire from the vicinity of the forklift. The wounded stormtrooper was again the target, and enough rounds found their mark to end the man's desperate crawl. He pitched face-first into the dirt and lay still.

Seeing the man gunned down before his eyes, Bolan was filled with a cold rage. He may have been unable to save his colleague, but he was determined to at least avenge the man's death.

Disregarding his own safety, the Executioner hauled himself onto electromagnetic crane's tanklike treads, then circled in front of the operator's cab to get at the crane's elongated swing arm. The gridlike framework provided him with hand- and footholds, allowing him to climb the strut as quickly as his strained hamstring would allow. He continued upward until he reached a point where he could peer down past the smoke. From his elevated position he now had a clear view of the sniper, positioned behind the forklift, tattooed arms gleaming in the flicker of nearby flames.

Anchoring himself with his legs and hips, Bolan pulled out his Beretta and dropped the foregrip. By the time he had the triad member in his sights, the man had spotted him as well and raised his AK-47.

Bolan won the race to the trigger. The gangster reeled back, dropping his rifle as he grabbed at his shoulder. He fell from view behind the forklift, but Bolan could hear the man shouting and knew he was still alive. Moments later more men came into view, firing at the remaining UN forces as they beelined toward the various entrances to the Quonset hut. Bolan drilled one of the men, then dropped a few rungs down the crane's rigging to avoid counterfire.

When the Executioner glanced back at the forklift, he saw the tattooed man stagger to safety inside the corrugated steel structure. One by one, the remaining gangsters followed suit.

Bolan started down the crane arm. Tetlock had warned him to stay clear of the compound, but he wasn't about to give the enemy a chance to regroup. He was going in after them.

The Executioner was clearing the last few rungs of the crane when his web holster snagged on an exposed bolt, causing him to lose his footing. When the holster's drawstring sheared, he felt himself free-falling. It was a short drop to the tread guard, but Bolan landed awkwardly and the air rushed from his lungs. He toppled over the crane chassis and landed on his knees in the dirt, dazed. It took him several moments to catch his breath and stand. By then he'd been joined by the two UN troopers who'd entered the grounds with him at the start of the siege.

"Looks like they want to play shootout at the O.K. Corral," one of the men said, eyes on the Quonset hut.

Bolan nodded and was about to lay out a plan for closing in on the gangsters when he caught himself and glanced skyward. He heard a strange, almost extraterrestrial sound, like the hum of a distant spaceship in a science-fiction movie. Bolan was familiar with the sound and, in a flash, he recalled part of Anthony Tetlock's earlier warning. *A jet...*

"Incoming!" Bolan shouted, reaching for the other two men and pulling them to the ground. They'd just hit the dirt when a one-ton, Paveway III-steered GBU-24 bomb slammed into the Quonset hut. The explosion that followed was so loud and blinding it seemed as if the sun itself had crashed to earth. Debris and shrapnel flew away from the fresh crater with the intensity of objects shooting out from a tornado. The outward force of the blast flattened most of the surrounding fence and sent both trucks and the Toyota Tercel tumbling across the ground like windblown bits of sagebrush. The forklift was close enough to the epicenter that it was lifted up and carried some twenty yards through the air before vanishing into the remains of the funeral pyre that had once been the trailer.

Outside the fence, Bolan waited for the last of the shrapnel to fly past, then slowly rose to his feet, shaken, ears ringing from the sound of the explosion. With equal tentativeness, the other two men pulled themselves from the ground.

"What the hell was that?" one of them cried out, staring at the smoldering maw where the Quonset hut had stood.

Bolan glanced up into the night air, not really expecting to see any sign of the F-14 that had delivered the precision strike.

"I have friends in high places," he said.

15

The crater was still aflame. Four firefighting units from the Jotuwi Port Authority had arrived and their thick, uncoiled hoses stretched like pythons around the blazing cavity as crews directed streams of water at the inferno. Sirens howled in the night and beacon lights flashed from atop the firetrucks, ambulances and law-enforcement vehicles crowding the lone access road leading to the heart of the salvage grounds.

On the main road, several police officers stood in front of patrol cars blocking the turnoff, trying, in vain, to keep traffic moving. Human nature being what it was, drivers couldn't resist the temptation to slow down for a better look at the aftermath of the firefight, and the slowdown had been compounded by a handful of minor collisions that had forced numerous vehicles onto the shoulder.

The various spot fires throughout the salvage yard had been doused, but smoke still rose from the charred shells of the two downed Kiowas. The workers' campfires had been doused and the authorities had corralled the yard's indigent work force into a clearing for questioning. Other police officers, armed with shotguns and flashlights, continued to roam the grounds, on the look for anyone—be it laborer or gangster—who might still be on the loose.

A swarm of news choppers circled overhead, capturing images of the carnage while trying to avoid colliding with one another. Some were cooperating with the police, aiding the search teams with their spotlights.

To Bolan, the proceedings seemed like a magnification of the grim circus that had unfolded in the jungle after the ambush carried out by Jiang Yang and his San Hop Kwan cohorts.

Yang had yet to turn up among the bodies that had been loaded into coroner vans or lined up in the dirt and covered with makeshift burlap shrouds pending the arrival of more body bags. Many of the victims, especially those gang members pulled from the hellhole created by the F-14's laser-guided bomb, had been burned beyond recognition and would require DNA swabs or dental records to be identified. Bolan knew Yang might well among the dead, but he, for one, would not rest until the man had been positively identified.

Bolan's hearing had yet to fully return and his hamstring was throbbing, but aside from slipping a chem-ice patch beneath the support sleeve around his leg, he'd forgone treatment from the paramedics on the scene, who had their hands full with the more seriously wounded. One of those patients, Anthony Tetlock, lay on a stretcher that had just been placed inside a Jotuwi Port Authority ambulance. The UN official was unconscious, and though the paramedics had stopped the flow of blood from his bullet wounds, they were worried that Tetlock had lost too much before they got to him. Even with an IV drip replenishing his system, the concern was that Tetlock would slip into an irreversible coma before they got him to the nearest hospital.

"Do the best you can," Bolan told the paramedics, barely able to hear the sound of his own voice.

His glance strayed to the gurney next to Tetlock, where the body of Bryce O'Shayne had already been zipped up inside a black neoprene bag. The toll had been high on both sides, he mused darkly. Besides himself and the two men with him at the time the laser-guided bomb had struck, only one other man from their team had survived the firefight. And four men had been all but vaporized inside the Kiowa Warriors.

Many more San Hop Kwan hardmen had been taken out than friendlies, but neither Bolan nor the other survivors felt any sense of triumph.

Bolan stepped back as the doors of the ambulance were closed. He watched it back up and slowly head up the entrance road, threading its way past the other vehicles. The Executioner kept working his jaw, trying to displace the pressure on his eardrums. Finally he heard and felt a pop in his right ear. Suddenly it felt as if someone had cranked up the volume on the activity taking place around him. The sirens, the shouting, the hiss of steam rising from the rocket crater: everything was louder, making the pandemonium even more immediate.

A paramedic from one of the other EMT vans saw Bolan limping and handed him a pair of crutches. "Here," the man said in faltering English. "It looks like you could use these."

Bolan waved off the offer at first, then relented. He knew putting excess weight on his bad leg wasn't helping matters, and the faster he could heal, the faster he could resume the battle against his newfound enemy.

When he tested the crutches, the jarring of the padded rests against his armpits somehow equalized the pressure in his left ear, restoring his hearing to near-full capacity. The stroke of good fortune also allowed him to make out a familiar voice calling out to him in the distance.

"Yo, Sarge!"

Bolan pivoted on the crutches and looked behind him. A military jeep pulled to a stop alongside one of the local police cruisers. Behind the wheel sat Jack Grimaldi, his hair tucked beneath a USS *Ronald Reagan* baseball cap. Sitting next to the Stony Man pilot was a taller, dark-haired man.

"Damn, is it good to see you!" John Kissinger called out as he and Grimaldi bounded from the jeep and joined Bolan.

"Likewise," Bolan said. Indicating the sunken caldron where the Quonset hut had stood, he added, "That was one hell of a lob you guys pitched."

Grimaldi shrugged. "Thanks, but it was technology all the way. All we did was pull the trigger."

"And we had our fingers crossed after that, I've got to tell you," Kissinger added. "We'd gotten word that everybody on our side had been warned to stay clear, but we had no way of knowing if your stuck with the program."

Bolan told his colleagues just how close he'd come to stepping into the line of fire, then asked, "How'd you manage to patch through a call to Tetlock?"

"Not our department," Grimaldi said. "The cyberguys back home were playing middleman the whole time. They were the ones in touch with Tetlock, passing along our ETA and whatnot."

"How is that guy, anyway?" Kissinger asked.

Bolan shook his head wearily. "It's not looking good." He quickly passed along the specifics.

"Sorry to hear that," Grimaldi said. "And your leg?"

"Hammy tweak," Bolan said. "Nothing to sweat over."

As the men made their way toward the crater, Grimaldi and Kissinger filled Bolan in on Phoenix Force's mission to Bali and how it had been prompted by the realization that their original targets had been taken into custody after the shootout earlier that evening in Jotuwi Port. Bolan, in return, laid out what had gone down at the salvage yard.

"I take it you saw them flock back into that Quonset hut before you triggered the GBU," the Executioner concluded.

Grimaldi nodded. "It wasn't an easy call, especially with the smoke blocking our view, but after the way they brought down those choppers, we didn't want to give them a chance to grab something else from their bag of tricks."

"Preemptive strike all the way," Kissinger said.

"You made the right call," Bolan said.

The men stopped a good twenty yards from the crater, held back by the snarl of fire hoses and the intense heat still emanating from the blast hole. There was an area where the fires had been put out, allowing a few men in bulky fire suits to cautiously inch their way down the muddy slope to look for more victims or survivors. The latter was an unlikely prospect, as nearly everything inside the crater had been reduced to glowing shards. A few of the larger pieces of machinery could still be detected amid the rubble.

As Bolan watched, the crew inside the crater was sent scrambling when a huge wall of water-saturated debris suddenly collapsed on itself. Some of the men were knocked to their knees as the slide spilled across the bottom of the incline.

"Whoa, check it out!" Grimaldi pointed to a section of the Quonset hut that had somehow remained intact throughout the bombing and subsequent fire. Shifting debris had undermined the floor slab, revealing an unexpected aspect to the hut's layout.

"A basement," Bolan said.

"That's not all," Kissinger replied.

One of the news crews in the overhead choppers had caught a glimpse of the slide and directed its searchlights into the crater. Even with all the smoke still rising from the hole, Bolan and the others were able to see the area that had fallen under the beam's harsh glow, and there could be no mistaking the man-made hole in the basement wall. In an instant, Bolan realized that perhaps the gangsters had retreated into the Quonset hut for a reason other than rearming themselves.

"An escape tunnel," he said.

16

At Bolan's request, the firefighting crews concentrated their hoses on the tunnel area, knocking down pockets of flame and using the pressurized flow of water to carve out a relatively unobstructed path along the bottom of the crater to the passageway. Grimaldi and Kissinger were among the first to climb down to the site. They'd advised Bolan to rest his leg and stay up top, but the Executioner had been unwilling to stand by idly, so he'd convinced the firefighters to lower him into the crater by means of one of the truck's fully extended, two-sectioned ladders. His Stony Man colleagues helped him off the ladder and once he'd secured himself on his crutches he followed them toward the tunnel.

The men had been given masks to ward off the possibility of inhaling toxic fumes, but the membrane filters could not fully block out the stomach-turning smell of scorched flesh and incinerated building materials.

"Not all that often you get a firsthand look at what's left after a GBU hits its mark," Kissinger said somberly, gaze falling on one of several drenched corpses yet to be retrieved from the debris. "Poor bastards never really had a chance."

"From the looks of it," Bolan countered, "if you guys had been a minute later with that bomb, they might've made it into the tunnel and gotten away."

Grimaldi had secured a high-powered flashlight from the

response crews, and when he shone its beam into the mouth of the six-foot-high tunnel, he and Kissinger could see the truth of Bolan's words. The walls of the underground passageway had been scorched by the fireball unleashed when the GBU-24 had detonated. Two gangsters lay facedown a few yards inside the tunnel, clothes burned from their backs, skin blackened by flames. When Kissinger turned over the bodies, Bolan recognized both men. One had been a purported confederate of Jiang Yang whose mug shot had been included in the files Tokaido had emailed prior to the assault. Bolan recognized the other as the man he'd traded shots with after he'd climbed up the arm of the electromagnetic crane. A few of the man's tattoos had been spared the blowtorchlike intensity of the bomb's flames and were still visible.

"I think that one's a Dai Lo," Bolan said. "He's the one who shouted for everyone to retreat to the hut just before you dropped the bomb."

"If that's the case," Grimaldi replied, "he was probably the first one into the tunnel."

The pilot shone his light ahead, revealing that the tunnel was empty for as far as they could see.

"We might as well follow it all the way, just in case," Kissinger said. He, like Grimaldi, had already unholstered his Colt Government Model 1911 pistol.

"Go ahead," said Bolan, backing up on his crutches. "I want to talk to some people up top about widening the search, because I think I know where this tunnel leads."

"Back to the port?" Kissinger asked.

Bolan shook his head. "You're turned around. This leads the other way. To the airport."

Jotuwi Regional Airport

JIANG YANG HAD LEARNED about the tunnel the first day he and his men had arrived in Malaysia to oversee the centrifuge transaction. They'd been offered lodging in a makeshift barracks in the basement beneath the Quonset hut, but the quarters were as cramped as the ventilation was poor, and halfway through their first night in Jotuwi, Yang and his colleagues had decided they'd rather not contend with the comingling body odors of their snoring Kuala Lumpur counterparts. The squalid accommodations in Lee-Kuan Mahr's trailer had been a meager upgrade, but Yang had weathered worse conditions in prison.

When he'd noticed the tunnel, one of Rhy Vhal's men had told them the passageway led to the airport and was used for transporting contraband to and from planes using a private hangar. Yang had made a mental note that the tunnel could also be useful as an escape route, and once the siege of the salvage yard had begun, his first thought had been to head underground.

As he taxied toward the runway at the controls of the same Raytheon Beechjet Hawker he'd flown to Jotuwi earlier in the week, Yang was glad he'd had the foresight to leave himself a ready out. From the runway, he could see the flurry of activity at the salvage grounds and guessed that his men as well as Vhal's had all been either killed or captured. He felt little remorse at having fled rather than stay behind and fight the enemy. Valor, in his mind, was overrated. It was better, he felt, to persevere.

Yang had received his pilot's license shortly before going to prison, and he'd logged a few hundred hours of flight time in the years since, more than enough time to learn not only the intricacies of flying but also how the aeronautics system worked and how it could be exploited to his benefit. He'd put that knowledge to use this night, using an alias when filing a hasty flight plan with the control tower. He'd manifested his destination as the Paracel Islands, a scattering of oversized coral reefs located just inside the Chinese maritime border between Hainan and the Spratly Islands. If need be, he would switch planes at the Paracels, but if he got the sense that he wasn't being tracked or followed, Yang figured he had enough fuel to make it all the way back to Hong Kong.

Once an aged Boeing 707 sped down the runway and lifted off into the heavens, Yang lined up his jet and awaited the go-ahead from the control tower. When the call came, the Dai Lo listened carefully to the air traffic controller's voice for any signs he was being coached by the authorities. Thankfully, the man sounded typically bored and officious. Yang acknowledged his clearance.

The jet rolled smoothly down the runway, picking up speed. Yang indulged himself with a faint smile as he felt the aircraft rise from the tarmac and carry him up into the night. He flew out over the waters of the Straits of Malacca, then banked slightly and swung the plane around. Soon he was flying directly over the salvage yard. Peering at the commotion below, his grin returned.

Twice he'd eluded his would-be captors. Twice he'd been woefully outnumbered and yet managed to cheat the odds and live to fight another day. It bode well for him, he figured. It seemed to him a sign that Destiny was watching over him, and that once back in Hong Kong, he would somehow find a way to escape Hu Dzem's wrath without having to play the ace up his sleeve.

I am chosen, he thought to himself, staring ahead at the moonlit horizon.

17

Hong Kong

Christine Wood was a fitness buff, and aside from walking the streets looking for Eva Kelmin she hadn't gotten any exercise since arriving in Hong Kong. So, after returning to her hotel, she turned her camera over to Molvico and went to the White Orchid's newly remodeled twenty-four-hour gym for a much-needed workout.

Molvico was going to feed Wood's digital photos of the Dynasty Club into a laptop in his room and use them for reference as he helped fellow agent Sam Chen finish blocking out a diagram of Hu Dzem's high-priced brothel. As Wood had asserted earlier, the more preparation they put into their next move, the better their chances of freeing Eva from her triad captors and putting her on the next plane back to San Francisco.

Given the late hour, the fitness center was fairly empty. Only a handful of diehards were at it with the free weights and cardio-vascular equipment. As part of the remodeling, the White Orchid had installed a rock-climbing facade along the entire north wall, where the ceiling pitched upward a good thirty feet from the fall mats. No one was using the vertical course, which consisted of stones and rocks imbedded in concrete dyed the color of sandstone, so Wood decided to forego her usual workout in favor of some climbing.

There were three routes up the wall, varying in degree of difficulty. Wood had taken up climbing a few months earlier, so she felt comfortable tackling the midrange course. When one of the staff members, an eighteen-year old Cantonese woman with a flawless English accent, came over to fit her with a safety harness, Wood waved away the contraption.

"I don't need that," she said.

"Sorry, but it's a regulation." The teenager, whose nametag read Suzi, pointed to a placard on the wall filled with more rules than there were amendments to the U.S. Constitution.

"If I fall, there's a safety mat, okay?" Wood said. "No big deal."

"It's a regulation," Suzi repeated. "For your own safety."

"Oh, come on," Wood protested. "You don't care about my safety. You're just trying to cover your ass legally."

"Perhaps," the young woman conceded.

"Look, I signed a waiver when I checked in," Wood said. "If you want, I'll add something about accepting responsibility if I do a header off the wall, okay? You guys will be off the hook, I'll enjoy myself and everyone will be happy."

Suzi glanced around to make sure no one was looking, then offered Wood a sly smile and confided, "Between you and me, I hate using a harness, too. Let me see what I can do."

"Atta girl," Wood replied, smiling back.

Suzi headed back toward the sign-in desk, pausing to help an older woman adjust the settings on her exercise bike. Something the woman said made Suzi laugh. Watching, Wood realized the staff worker was probably the same age as Eva Kelmin.

The thought filled her with a sudden rush of sadness. Eva wasn't the first runaway Wood had encountered who'd wound up caught up in a life of prostitution. She'd been on a few similar assignments, and in every instance she'd managed to return the runaway to her family, only to learn later that the teenager had been irreparably changed by her experience, and never for the better. One young woman had wound up in drug rehab after turning to heroin as a way to forget her ordeal. Another had resumed turning tricks and fallen through the cracks after being disinherited. A third young woman had taken up joyriding in stolen cars and been killed after losing control of her vehicle in a police chase.

One way or another, Wood feared that Eva was doomed for a similar fate and would never, like Suzi, be able to go through life with an easy smile or a flair for innocent laughter. That most likely had already been taken from her.

Wood was stretching when Suzi returned with a clipboard. Apparently a number of guests had issues with the safety harness, because Wood's waiver had been rubber-stamped with an addendum asserting that she'd tackle the rock wall at her own risk. She quickly initialed the clause and handed the clipboard back.

"Thanks, Suzi."

"No problem," Suzi replied, smiling. "Enjoy."

Wood was about to start up the wall when a middle-aged man sauntered over from the free weights, toweling sweat from his forehead.

"Hey, sweetcake—" his voice boomed at Suzi with a Texas accent "—time for Spider-Man to kick into action. Unless you're off work soon, of course, in which case I can think of something else to climb besides this wall here, if you catch my drift."

Wood rolled her eyes, leaving Suzi to contend with the blowhard. She normally used special shoes for rock climbing, but her workout sneakers were flexible and had enough tread to allow her to make her way up the rock facing with minimal difficulty. She was in no hurry, preferring to take her time and feel the exertion on each muscle group as she moved from rock to rock.

"You wanna speed it up, there, lady?" a voice called out.

Wood looked over her shoulder and saw the Texan a few yards below her on the wall. He'd strapped on the safety harness, allowing him to move with less concern about falling.

"Excuse me?" Wood said.

"Hey, no offense," the Texan said, flashing a few thousand dollars' worth of capped teeth. "I'm liking the view and all, but how about stepping aside and letting a man through?"

"If you see one, let me know," Wood shot back.

"Ooh, feisty," the Texan drawled. "I like that in a woman."

"What matchbox university are you getting your material from, anyway?" Wood asked, holding her ground.

"Hey, I save my best material for the bedroom." The Texan winked suggestively. "Interested?"

Wood reached to her right for a handhold and swung herself over to the more difficult facing, then gestured to the Texan. "The runway's clear, Casanova. Go for it."

"I'll take that for a no."

"Very perceptive."

The Texan shrugged. "Your loss, sweetheart."

Wood stayed put, letting the Texan huff and puff his way past her. A few more yards up the facing and he began to slow down, winded. Wood smiled and turned her focus to the more difficult course she'd stepped onto. With relative ease, she climbed her way upward, passing the Texan, who'd come to a stop ten yards from the summit.

"Want me to call for an ambulance?" she called out to him.

The Texan glared at her, still catching his breath. "Bitch," he managed to gasp.

"That must be the A material you were talking about."

"Fuck you."

"You wish."

Seething, the Texan reached up, determined to beat Wood the rest of the way up the facing. Wood bounded up a full length ahead of him, then suddenly swung her left leg out and set her foot on the same rock the Texan had just grabbed.

"Yeow!" The Texan lost his footing and tumbled backward, quickly using up the slack on his safety harness. The next thing he knew, he was dangling helplessly in midair, flailing his arms and legs as if he were doing an impression of the world's worst swimmer. He directed a few more choice curses Wood's way, but she'd already turned her back to him and was scaling the last few yards to a narrow landing atop the wall. Once there, she sat on the edge and stared past the Texan, waving to Suzi, who was doing her best not to laugh at the tourist's predicament.

"I don't know, Suzi," Wood called down. "I don't think this one's a keeper, so you might have to throw him back."

SHOWERED AND CHANGED, Wood dropped her gym bag in her room and then went next door to check on Molvico and Chen.

Sam Chen was a tall, lanky Chinese American with a crew cut and goatee. He was posted at the window overlooking Hennessey Avenue, peering through acacia trees at the Dynasty Club.

"Anything exciting?" Wood asked.

Chen shook his head faintly. "Pretty dead over there."

"Nothing turned up on the photos, either," Molvico called out from the dining-room table, where his attention was divided between his laptop and a room-service order of chow mein and chicken salad. "Just a few tweaks for the layout diagram."

Wood joined Molvico, helping herself to a sprig of lettuce. On the laptop screen was a computer-rendered overhead view of the Dynasty's second floor, mostly taken from building permits Inter-Trieve had managed to get their hands on the previous day. Based on a few firsthand accounts from brothel clients who were part of the agency's informant pool, Molvico had marked which rooms were used for trysts and which were set aside for other triad business.

It wasn't indicated on the diagram, but Molvico and Chen had already learned of the pecking order that allowed more civilized clients to use the outer rooms while deviants wound up in the windowless quarters set back from the street.

Molvico had just finished adding the alley fire escape to the diagram and designating the front balcony entrances as sliding glass doors.

"What about that couple I took a shot of?" Wood asked.

Molvico held one hand out and gave a so-so gesture.

"I'll show you the blow-up, but there's not much detail."

Molvico called up the photo in question. He'd used the computer's software to zoom in on the couple embracing behind the thin shades. A few photo-enhancing tools had, in effect, peeled away the shades but failed to reveal any distinguishing facial characteristics. But judging from the woman's height and posture, Wood was pretty certain it wasn't Eva Kelmin.

"She's gotta be in there somewhere," Wood said.

"With any luck, we'll find out tomorrow," Molvico said.

The twinge of sadness Wood had felt earlier returned. She went to the window and stood alongside Chen, staring out at the brothel.

"Hang in there, kiddo," she whispered. "Help is on the way."

18

Eva Kelmin had one more client, a forty-year-old electronics executive who stank of cigarettes and had secret dreams of being a stand-up comedian. For nearly an hour he'd bored Eva senseless with a seemingly endless series of lame jokes he'd gotten off the Internet earlier in the night. His choice of material was juvenile at best, and he was so inept with his delivery that Eva had found it even more challenging to be a good audience than to physically satisfy him.

Her nightly ordeal finished, Eva sat in her bathtub, immersed in suds and hot water, trying to put her dilemma behind her and quiet her mind so that she might have some chance of getting a good night's sleep. Along with the other lessons picked up during her captivity, Eva had learned that life at the Dynasty was easier to deal with when she was well-rested.

The shower stall surrounding the bathtub was lined with ten-inch faux marble tiles. As she had many nights before, Eva picked out a random tile and tried to see something in the whorls and swirls, much the way she and her mother used to lie on the grass back home in San Francisco and amuse themselves making the clouds overhead morph into everything from clowns to overweight ballerinas. Back then the pastime had been more innocent, an end unto itself. Now, it was a coping mechanism.

At first Eva's imagination failed her, but eventually a figure emerged out of the would-be marble, materializing with such sudden clarity that she let out an involuntary gasp and closed her eyes, trying to will the image away. When she opened her eyes, the figure remained: a shrouded Grim Reaper with hunched shoulders holding a blunt-edged scythe. There was no face visible beneath the hood, merely a dark blotch, and yet Eva found herself shuddering, filled with a sense that malevolent eyes were trained on her. She closed her eyes again and sank lower in the tub, feeling the suds brush up against her chin.

No matter how hard she tried, however, she was unable to shake the image from her mind. And, as disturbing as the image was in and of itself, what the Reaper signified to Eva filled her with even greater horror. The image of the cowled figure took her back to the day of her mother's funeral. That gray, drizzling Saturday four years earlier, she'd overheard her aunts talking and had learned for the first time that, contrary to what her father had told her, her mother had died from an overdose of sleeping pills. "I knew her demons would get to her sooner or later," Eva's aunt Janice had whispered.

Eva had pretended she hadn't overheard the conversation, but secretly she'd taken it upon herself to investigate her mother's death. Two days after the funeral, she'd carefully searched the sunroom where Mandy Kelmin had spent so many hours staring out at the one lone spire of the Golden Gate Bridge visible above the neighboring rooftops. In a hollow cavity beneath the coffee table Eva found a journal and read with morbid fascination about her mother's long battle with depression—something Eva had never even been aware of. Her mother had written of voices that haunted her, constantly telling her there was only one way to end her pain. She'd finally begun to refer to her phantom counselor as the Reaper. In the last entry in the journal, dated the morning before she'd killed herself, Eva's mother had written: *The Reaper says tomorrow is the day. Thank you, Reaper.*

Recalling that nightmare, Eva let out a sudden sob that echoed loudly off the tiled walls of the shower enclosure. Tears were streaming down her cheeks and, staring past the soap bubbles surrounding her, she could see a snakelike stream of blood rising up through the water from her right hand. She pulled her hand from the water and saw that she'd dug her nails so deeply into the palm of her hand that she'd broken the skin.

Eva blinked away her tears and stared at the blood trickling from the self-inflicted wound, then glanced back at the tiled wall. The Reaper was still there, camouflaged by the faux marble. She realized it wasn't a scythe that he was holding, but rather a razor, like the one she used to shave her legs.

The razor was resting in a plastic soap dish at the foot of the tub. When she leaned forward to reach for it, she eyed the wall tiles again. Up this close, the Reaper seemed to disappear, lost in the random patterns of the fake stone. But when she leaned back, razor in hand, the apparition reappeared. As she continued to stare at the wall, she stopped weeping. Slowly, a strange calm began to settle over her.

Maybe her mother had sent the Reaper for her, she thought to herself. Was that it? Was her mother calling out to her? It made sense. Her mother had always looked after her, always tried to make things right in her world, always offered comfort in her time of need. Maybe that's what she was doing now. Maybe her mother had sent the Reaper to show her a way out of this hell.

"Mom?" Eva whispered faintly, looking around the sparsely furnished bathroom. Her kimono lay haphazardly over the sink and there was a hairbrush on the ledge below the mirror, but otherwise there was nothing in the bathroom but a lone towel hanging from a hook behind the door.

"Mommy?" Eva called out, raising her voice slightly. "Mommy, are you here?"

Eva was answered by silence. All she could hear was the slight rippling of the bathwater and the faint popping of soap bubbles. Her palm had stopped bleeding, but the crimson trail had trickled down to her wrist, almost like an arrow pointing out a twin pair of bluish veins. Eva stared at the veins, then pressed her fingertips against them until she could feel her pulse. Her gaze went back to the tiles and the ever-clearer image of the Reaper.

She drew in a deep breath, then let it out slowly and placed the razor over the inside of her wrist. She pressed down slightly and could feel the steel blades nipping at her skin.

LI CHUANNAN'S GUN didn't need cleaning, but the Dynasty bouncer was restless and had to do something to make the time pass. There was still one client at the club—a bondage freak doing something that involved using straps and duct tape on one of the low-rent girls working out of the inner rooms—and Chuannan couldn't leave until the man had finished.

He fussed over his 8-round Tokarev TT-33, a lightweight KGB hand-me-down that seemed almost toylike in his large hands. He was still up in Hu Dzem's penthouse office, and periodically he glanced at the surveillance monitors, making sure the bondage freak didn't get carried away. It'd been a few weeks since Chuannan had wound up with a body on his hands after a prostitute had been overly roughed up, and he was in no mood to go driving through the city with a corpse in his trunk, looking for a place to get rid of it.

What Chuannan really wanted to do was go out drinking. And he wasn't interested in just pouring back a few cold ones. He wanted to get stinking drunk and then get into a fight with some chump and vent all the steroid-fueled rage that had been building up inside him since Hu Dzem had hinted that he might be called on to take out Jiang Yang; provided, of course, that his drinking buddy made it back from Malaysia in one piece.

Chuannan didn't like the way things were shaping up. Soon, he realized, the time would come for him to make a choice between allegiances, and much as he wanted to side with Jiang Yang, deep down there was a part of Chuannan that realized Yang's high-minded talk about displacing Hu Dzem might amount to nothing. If Chuannan made the wrong choice, he'd not only lose the privileges and easy lifestyle that came with being Dzem's prized goon, he might also wind up in a trunk himself.

Chuannan was extracting a bristle brush from the barrel of his Tokarev when Hu Dzem's shrill voice filled the room.

"She can't do that!" The chairman dropped the phone he'd been whispering into and rushed out from behind his desk, nearly bowling over his two bodyguards. "Stop her!"

Startled, Chuannan looked up from his gun, checking the monitor where the bondage freak's prostitute lay on her bed, bound but not showing any sign of being in danger.

"Not her!" Dzem railed, pointing at a different monitor with his ringed index finger. "Her!"

Li Chuannan shifted his gaze. Another spycam situated in Eva Kelmin's bathroom showed the teenager pressing a razor to her wrist while sitting naked in the bathtub. Alarmed, the bouncer rose to his feet and headed for the door. Before he could reach it, Dzem, eyes still fixed on the monitor, waved for him to stop. "Wait, wait," he called out. "She put it down."

Chuannan stopped and glanced back at the chairman and his bodyguards. Both goons were struggling to keep a straight face. To them, Hu Dzem was merely indulging in another of his high-strung fits. Chuannan suspected that once they were off duty and by themselves, both men would have a good laugh at their boss's expense. The bouncer didn't care for either man, and part of him hoped that Hu Dzem would catch them sniggering. But he was in no mood for any more of the chairman's histrionics and decided instead to diffuse the situation.

"Maybe I should still check on her," he suggested.

"No!" Dzem exclaimed. "Leave her alone!"

Chuannan chafed at the rebuke and glared at Dzem, who continued to watch Eva, who was now getting out of the tub and reaching for a towel. As the girl toweled herself off, Chuannan stared carefully at the chairman, who, in turn, remained transfixed by the sight of Eva. Chuannan figured she was young enough to be Dzem's granddaughter, and yet here he was, eyes as filled with predatory desire as any pedophile. It finally dawned the bouncer why Dzem was keeping the girl captive instead of contacting her father about a ransom.

Several times Dzem had coyly shrugged off the idea, claiming they could ask for more money if they gave Scott Kelmin more time to miss his daughter. But the real reason, Chuannan now realized, was that Dzem found some perverse satisfaction in having Eva turn tricks under his clandestinely watchful eye, especially after he dictated the terms for their sexual congress. Jiang Yang had often claimed that Dzem was impotent, and Chuannan was beginning to think there was some truth to it.

Maybe Dzem had to content himself with voyeurism and let surrogates carry out the acts he was no longer capable of. It would certainly explain his not wanting Chuannan to burst into the girl's room so quickly after she'd nearly attempted suicide. Dzem clearly didn't want Eva to know about the hidden cameras.

Sick, Chuannan thought to himself. The chairman was sick. And pathetic. He'd shown himself to be far less than an all-powerful tyrant. Having lowered his guard, Hu Dzem had exposed a vulnerability, an Achilles' heel Chuannan could exploit.

Several times Jiang Yang had suggested that it might become necessary for Chuannan to take out the chairman. Each time, Chuannan had been secretly terrified by the notion. Hu Dzem, despite his buffoonery, was too formidable a target.

No more. Watching the chairman ogle Eva as she slipped

into her kimono, Chuannan realized for the first time it might indeed be possible for him to kill the chairman and live to tell the tale. Better yet, he had an idea how he might go about it.

19

Stony Man Farm, Virginia

"Your gut deserves a medal," Barbara Price told Hal Brognola. "Sending Jack and Cowboy to help Striker was definitely the right call."

"Never underestimate the value of a good hunch," Brognola said.

The two officials were still in the Annex Computer Room, monitoring the situation in Jotuwi. Grimaldi and Kissinger were checking with airport security to see if Jiang Yang had fled there from the salvage grounds. Meanwhile, Bolan had stopped by the airfield's medical facilities to check on the condition of Anthony Tetlock. The UN officer was in surgery. Bolan had asked the Farm to run a check on any possible ties the triad might have with the airport. The task had fallen to Akira Tokaido, and when Price and Brognola stopped by his workstation, he had news for them.

"Besides the main terminal, there are a few privately owned hangars," Tokaido reported. "It took some digging, but I got a search to cough up what we're looking for."

"San Kwan Hop owns one of the hangars?" Price asked.

"Affirmative," Tokaido said. "It's jointly owned. One firm is traceable back to Hu Dzem in Hong Kong. The other's a shell outfit run by a Hop crew in Kuala Lumpur.

Probably the same guys running the salvage yard operation."

"Good work," Brognola told Akaido. "You pass along word to Striker?"

Tokaido nodded. "He already got the e-mail. My guess is he's making a house call as we speak..."

Jotuwi Regional Airport, Malaysia

THE PRIVATE HANGARS were on the opposite side of the runways from the main terminal. Bolan didn't want to lose time tracking down Grimaldi and Kissinger, so he quickly commandeered a trio of police officers lingering outside the medical facility. He rode shotgun in one of the squad cars while the other two cops followed in a second cruiser, circling around the runway. As they came upon the hangar Tokaido had specified in his e-mail, the two vehicles split off, the second car heading behind the building while Bolan's cruiser pulled to a stop in front.

"They had to see us coming," Bolan said, pulling out his Beretta. "No point playing it close to the vest."

The moment he stepped out of the cruiser, Bolan knew they'd come to the right place. One of the mechanics inside the service bay closest to him had reached into his toolbox, swapping a torque wrench for a pistol, which he put to quick use, plugging Bolan's door with one slug and just missing the Executioner's face with another.

Bolan crouched behind the door, using it for cover, and returned fire. The Beretta's triple-header caught the mechanic in the chest and the gunman reeled forward, toppling his toolbox before slumping to the concrete. Another mechanic ducked under the fuselage of the Piper Cub he was servicing, heading to flee out the rear exit. When he threw the door open, however, the second squad car had already pulled up, blocking his retreat. He fumbled at his waistband for a Walther PPK, but before he could bring the gun into play he caught rounds from a service revolver and let out a cry, dropping in his tracks.

Bolan charged into the hangar. The man he'd shot bore no resemblance to Jiang Yang, so he quickly resumed his search, circling around the Piper Cub and heading for the office area. Someone had just slammed the door shut on him, and Bolan figured the lock had been thrown, as well.

"Give me a hand!" he shouted to the cop who'd driven him to the hangar. Together, they put their weight against a rolling cast-iron engine hoist, shoving the contraption toward the door. Chains rattled and wheels creaked as the half-ton hoist rolled across the grease-stained floor, picking up momentum. The door was solid-cored oak, but neither it nor the dead bolt could hold up against the force of the hoist. With a deafening crunch, the door splintered open, even as the bolt sheared through the jamb.

Bolan helped the cop shove the hoist the rest of the way into the office, using it for cover. The man who'd closed the door on them had retreated behind a file cabinet. He fired his pistol twice, bouncing slugs off the hoist, then tossed the gun aside and threw his arms up in surrender as he stepped clear of the cabinet. He was a short man in his fifties. Not Jiang Yang.

The Executioner kept his Beretta trained on the man as he moved forward. He asked the police officer to translate for him, then told their prisoner, "You know why we're here. Talk fast, and when your lips move they better be telling the truth."

The hangar was secured, but in searching the premises, the police left one stone unturned. During the initial exchange of gunfire, Choi Peng, a young San Kwan Hop recruit from Kuala Lumpur, had fled to the utility room containing the hangar's heating and air-conditioning unit as well a storage cabinet filled with propane tanks and welding equipment. There was a small crawl space between the cabinet and the rear wall, and Peng had managed to squeeze his small frame into the cavity. The police had searched the room as well as the storage cabinet, but they'd bypassed the crawl space.

Trembling, Peng remained in his hiding place, straining to hear what was going on over the mad pounding of his heart. Minutes passed. The youth nearly gave himself away when a spider crawled up his leg, causing him to shudder, in the process rattling the cabinet. No one came to investigate, however. Still, Peng stayed put, waiting until he felt his legs beginning to cramp up on him before squeezing out from behind the cabinet. He was sweating and he'd drawn blood where he'd scraped his arm against the back side of the cabinet. But he was alive and, at least for the moment, he was free.

Peng knew why the police had come, and he also guessed they had probably taken at least one of the other workers alive. If anyone had talked, the authorities knew that Jiang Yang had come to the hangar from the salvage yard before taking off in the Beechjet. Peng knew that somehow he had to warn Yang that the cops were on to him.

"VERY SORRY."

Davi Jaan, head of security operations at Jotuwi Regional Airport, eyed Jack Grimaldi and John Kissinger with a look that was part frustration, part embarrassment. The three men were standing in the waiting area of the man's headquarters, a bungalow situated between the international terminal and the airport runways. Through the open doorway behind them, smoke could still be seen rising from the nearby salvage grounds.

"We have checked the terminal," the Malay official reported, "and there are no reports of suspicious activity."

"What about surveillance cameras?" Kissinger asked.

Jaan shrugged. "We have looked through all the footage of passengers boarding planes over the past two hours. No one matches the description of the man you are looking for."

"He might've disguised himself," Grimaldi suggested.

"I don't think so," Kissinger interjected. "The way things went down, I don't see him having time for anything like that."

"My men are still checking the private hangars," Jaan offered. "Perhaps they will come up with something."

"Let's hope so," Kissinger said. "We could use a break."

"Isn't there a chance this man is still back at the salvage yard?" Jaan asked. "It's a large area, and you said yourselves that not all of the bodies have been identified yet."

"Yeah, that's possible," Kissinger said, "but we came across a set of fresh footprints in the tunnel leading from there to here. Our money says it's Yang."

One of Jaan's junior officers called out from a back room, saying he was needed on a matter unrelated to the search for Jiang Yang. Jaan excused himself. Moments after he disappeared into the back room, Mack Bolan entered the bungalow, his features molded into a look of solemnity.

"How's Tetlock?" Kissinger asked.

Bolan stared at Kissinger. His expression spoke volumes, bracing the Stony Man weaponsmith for the worst.

"He didn't make it," Bolan responded gravely. "He went into arrest while in surgery. They couldn't bring him back."

"Damn," Kissinger muttered.

"He was one of the good ones," Bolan said.

Grimaldi nodded. "I know it's not much consolation, but whoever took him out is probably roasting in a hell worse than the one we cooked up with that laser-guided bomb."

When Bolan didn't respond, Kissinger changed the subject. "No news on Yang. Security checked around but came up empty."

"I had some luck on that front," the Executioner said.

Bolan told his colleagues how he'd followed up on Akira Tokaido's information about San Hop Kwan owning one of the airport's private hangars. He filled them in on the brief skirmish at the hangar, then checked his watch and gave them the bottom line.

"According to the guy we questioned, Yang flew out an hour ago in the same jet he used to fly his crew here from Hong Kong."

JIANG YANG PUSHED the jet to its limit, coaxing it up to more than five hundred miles an hour. He knew it meant he'd be running on fumes by the time he reached Hong Kong, but he wanted to get back as quickly as possible so that he could start working his spin on the debacle in Malaysia. The bravado he'd felt in the moments after fleeing Jotuwi had been tempered by the realization that once the news reached his colleagues in China, he would be hard-pressed to save face, much less advance his stature within the triad.

But he had to make the effort. What other option was there? He'd had the foresight to court another ally, but if he went to them now he'd have no bargaining position. They would know he'd come to them out of desperation and would treat him accordingly. He knew he had to wait for a better opportunity. More to the point, he had to wait until he could meet the one crucial condition his prospective ally had insisted on—the murder of Hu Dzem.

Until such time as he could arrange the chairman's death, Yang knew he would have to do what he could to make things right with his mentor and the rest of San Hop Kwan. It was that simple.

Yang had radioed a change to his flight plan, claiming it was necessary because his instrumentation was acting up. He'd reported that he was steering clear of the South China Sea in favor of a slightly more beeline course across the Gulf of Thailand and the peninsular landmass of Cambodia, Laos and Vietnam. He'd said he wanted to stay as close to land as possible in case he needed to attempt an emergency landing, but the truth was that he figured the rerouting would shave thirty minutes off his flight. With his future—and perhaps his life—at stake, he knew every second counted.

Passing over Da Nang, Yang could see the glittering black waters of the Gulf of Tonkin and, less than a hundred miles away, a sprinkling of lights along the southern coastline of Hainan Island. Hong Kong was, at most, an hour's flight away.

Yang was halfway across the gulf when any delusions he had escaped Malaysia undetected were burst by a frantic radio dispatch from Choi Peng, the triad flunky who'd managed to slip away when authorities had descended on the syndicate's private hangar back in Jotuwi. The man told Yang that those same authorities had just learned from another worker about the gangster's getaway. "They know you are headed back to Hong Kong," the informant concluded.

Yang cursed, then asked, "What else?"

"They're coming after you," came the reply.

"In what?" Yang said. "What are they flying?"

"Fighter jets," Peng told him. "F-14s. Two of them are on the runway waiting to take off."

Yang cursed again. He knew the Tomcats were three times as fast as his jet. Yang did some quick math and realized there was a chance the F-14s would catch up to him before he reached Hong Kong. And even if they didn't, an order had probably been sent out, meaning there could well be other aircraft closer to his position taking to the air to intercept him. The Hawker was unarmed, meaning Yang would not have the option of taking on any pursuers.

"Do they know I changed my flight course?" Yang asked.

"I don't know," Peng confessed.

"Find out and get back to me," Yang said.

The moment he ended the call, Yang was overcome with paranoia, wondering if his conversation had somehow been picked up by the enemy. The more he thought about it, the more he became convinced they were on to him, tracking his every movement. Working the plane's controls, he quickly disabled the plane's transponders. It would make the aerial search for him more difficult, but Yang suspected he was only forestalling the inevitable. Sooner or later, they would find him.

"Think!" he exhorted himself. "There has to be a way out of this!"

As he brainstormed, Yang kept pushing the Beechjet, taking the jet's speed to 530 miles per hour. Up ahead, Hainan Island loomed larger with each passing second, almost beckoning. The Dai Lo stared at the island and slowly realized that beyond providing him with a shortcut to Hong Kong, his detour had unwittingly presented him with a way out of his newfound predicament. It would require playing his trump card under unfavorable circumstances, but given the alternatives, it seemed clear Destiny was once again calling the shots for him, telling Yang that it was time for last resorts.

Once he'd resolved what he had to do, Yang grew calm. This just might work, he thought to himself.

There was one matter left to attend to. Taking one hand from the controls, Yang fished through his pockets for his cell phone. He turned it on, then drew in a deep breath, waiting to see if he was within service range. He knew there was a chance any call he made might be intercepted, but it seemed more likely the enemy was, if anything, tracking his radio transmissions. The cell phone might well be secure enough for him to put into motion a dormant plan that would allow him to meet the terms set forth by his intended new ally.

Provided, of course, that Li Chuannan picked up the call.

Hong Kong

LI CHUANNAN HAD LEFT the Dynasty and was heading down Hennessey Avenue for the nearest bar when his cell phone vibrated in his coat pocket. He was craving a drink and his first thought was to ignore the call, but when he checked the display after the third ring and recognized Yang's number, he quickly brought the cell to his ear.

"You're alive," he said. "I was worried when I heard—"

"Listen to me!" Yang interrupted. "I can't talk long, but there's something I need you to do."

Chuannan strode past the noise spilling out of the bar, plugging his left ear so that he could better hear Yang. There seemed to be some kind of interference on the line. That or Yang was talking from inside a train or some other loud vehicle.

"Where are you?" he asked.

"Never mind that!" Yang told him. "It's time to make our move. The one we discussed involving Hu Dzem. Are you with me?"

Chuannan fell silent, stunned. This was it. One way or another, he had to make a decision. He had to choose sides.

"Are you there?" Yang shouted in his ear. "I need an answer!"

Chuannan let out a breath, then told Yang, "I'm with you."

"I knew I could count on you." Yang sounded only partially relieved. He went on, "How soon can you do it?"

Chuannan's mind raced. He wanted to ask more questions, but from the urgency in Yang's voice he doubted he would get any answers. At least not until Hu Dzem was taken care of.

Chuannan tried to think. The chairman had just left the Dynasty with his bodyguards. He had a late meeting somewhere across town, then would be heading back to his home, a veritable fortress across the bay in Kowloon. There was no way Chuannan could get to him there.

"I need an answer!" Yang repeated.

"In the morning," Chuannan told his colleague. "I can get to him when he comes in for work."

"Do it, then!" Yang told him. "Call me when it's done!"

"Where will you be?" Chuannan asked.

Yang didn't respond. The line went dead in the bouncer's ear. Chuannan slowly lowered the phone. His hands were shaking and his forehead had broken out in a sweat. He turned and glanced back at the bar. A hawker out front grinned at him.

"Come in," he said. "You look like you could use a drink."

Li Chuannan stared at the man and shook his head, then strode past the bar, tracing his steps back to the Dynasty. The drinking would have to wait.

20

Blistering through the night sky at a speed of nearly 1600 miles an hour, Jack Grimaldi brought his loaner F-14 Tomcat within visual contact of Yang's luxury jet some thirty-six thousand feet above the southern coast of Hainan Island. Below the fighter jet, through a thin patchwork of clouds, tight clusters of light could be seen out on the South China Sea, marking derrick facilities servicing the underwater gas line that ran from the coastal resort city of Sanya all the way to Hong Kong.

"Closing in," Grimaldi called out over his radio headset.

"Gotcha," Kissinger replied from his position directly behind the Grimaldi. For the past hour he'd been trying to make radio contact with Yang. "Guy's still not taking any calls."

"Well, another minute or two and we'll be close enough to knock on his door," Grimaldi said jokingly.

"That or knock it down," Kissinger countered, letting his gaze stray to the Tomcat's HUD. Flicking a few switches, Kissinger soon had the Beechjet in his target sights. The F-14 had a pair of Sparrow missiles mounted to its underbelly along with two Sidewinders, and a 20 mm Vulcan cannon was housed just above the fighter jet's nosewheels.

Yang's aircraft, on the other hand, was armed only with its overpriced entertainment system. There would be no dogfight. Yang would either surrender or face the same kind of obliteration his counterparts, had visited upon the two Kiowa helicopters at the Jotuwi salvage grounds.

As the gap narrowed between the two aircraft, Grimaldi slowed and switched on his navigational flashers, then veered slightly to the left, planning to ease slightly ahead of the Beechjet and then rock his wings to signal to Yang that he'd been intercepted. Once he'd pulled alongside the other plane, however, the Stony Man pilot realized there was no point in going through any warning maneuver.

"About that door we were going to knock on," he told Kissinger. "There's a slight problem."

Kissinger drew his attention away from the HUD and glanced out the canopy to his right. "Whoa," he murmured. "No way."

To both men's amazement, the Beechjet's boarding doorway, located directly behind the cockpit, gaped wide open, revealing the faint interior lights of the passenger cabin.

"No wonder we couldn't make radio contact," Grimaldi said. "That bastard went on autopilot and jumped."

Hainan Island, China

IT WAS MORE THAN MERE marketing savvy that the led developers of Hainan Island to refer to its southern coastline as The Hawaii of the Orient. The long-stretching beaches offered the same fine-grained white sand, and the omnipresent coconut palms, thatch-roofed bungalows and gently lapping waves seemed the perfect backdrop for an evening luau. In fact, just such a luau was taking place a short stroll downhill from the casino and main tower of the Feike Shoals Resort, a fifty-five-acre getaway paradise located an hour's drive from the tourist congestion of Sanya. Drinks were flowing, a suckling pig was being roasted over a fiery pit, and a chorus line of Chinese beauties in hula skirts were undulating to the music of legendary Hawaiian crooner Don Ho. All this part of the "free" entertainment for high rollers ponying up thousands of dollars a night for one of the resort's thirty-seven beachfront luxury suites.

Tuxedoed security agents were posted at the entrance to the beach area, checking IDs to make sure no one crashed the party. More guards, dressed in cotton shorts and Hawaiian print shirts, roamed barefoot along the tide line, on the lookout for more industrious outsiders who might attempt to paddle their way to the festivities. There was one point of entry they had neglected to take into account, however, and a sudden clamor arose among the partygoers. Eyes were cast skyward and fingers pointed to a lone figure drifting toward them, dangling beneath a mushroom-shaped parachute. Most of the guests—a mix of Westerners, Australians and Asians—thought it was part of the entertainment.

The security detail knew better, however, and by the time Jiang Yang had touched down in the shallow surf, four guards had him surrounded, guns drawn.

"Don't shoot!" Yang pleaded as he struggled to his feet, grappling with his harness. The parachute had collapsed in the water and when the tide attempted to pull it out to sea, Yang was jerked off balance and fell back into the surf. Finally he managed to free himself of the harness and stand up.

The guards quickly frisked Yang, exchanging glances with one another as they came across the Dai Lo's Glock pistol and fighting chain. The weapons were confiscated, and Yang's right arm was twisted behind his back by one of the guards.

"Let me explain!" Yang cried out.

"You'll explain, all right, but not here!"

Two guards brusquely escorted Yang ashore while the others did their best to gather up the parachute, which seemed to be fighting them off like the mother of all jellyfish. Meanwhile, the resort's director of special engagements had rushed to the stage and gestured for the band to resume playing. The guests were still preoccupied with the sight of Yang being brought into custody.

The gangster at first struggled with the guards and tried once more to get in a word on his behalf, but with all the noise and commotion he realized it was pointless, so he finally complied and allowed himself to be led past the stage and fire pit to the lei-festooned archway leading the neon-pulsing facade of the casino. Halfway up the walk, Yang stopped. "Listen to me!" he demanded, holding his free hand out so the guards could get a good look at it in the glow of well-placed security lights.

One of the guards was getting out his handcuffs and the other was about to twist Yang's arm tighter behind his back when they both recognized the telltale dragon tattoo enveloping Yang's wrist and the back of his hand. The first guard took a step back and clipped the handcuffs back onto his waist strap. The other released Yang and likewise moved away from the drenched gangster. The contempt in their eyes had been replaced by a wary respect and no small measure of fear.

"Why are you here?" one of them asked. "We have no quarrel with the triads."

"I'm here to see Ki Dan," Yang answered, referring to the reclusive Chinese billionaire whose financial holdings included, amongst other things, the Feike as well as more than half of the other resorts dotting the Hainan Island coastline.

"He's not here," one of the guards responded.

"Where is he?" Yang asked.

"In the Philippines," the guard told him. "On business."

Yang was taken aback. "When is he due back?"

"In the morning."

"It's important that I see him," Yang persisted. "There must be a way for you to reach him."

"In the case of an emergency, we can—"

"This *is* an emergency!" Yang interrupted. "Call him! Tell him Jiang Yang is here to see him. He'll know what it's about."

"ONE MORE PASS," Bolan called through his headset to Lieutenant William Smith, the pilot of the second F-14 Tomcat pursuing Jiang Yang. Smith, a twenty-three-year-old California native twelve months into his four-year stint with the Navy, nodded and banked the fighter jet, preparing to drop another few thousand feet as he arced out over the coastal waters off Hainan Island. He'd already flown over the area twice while Bolan, riding behind him, had tried to use the Tomcat's advanced targeting resources to pinpoint where Jiang Yang might have landed after bailing from his Beechjet Hawker in midflight.

Unfortunately, while the thirty million dollar fighter jet was nearly unsurpassed when it came to homing in on established targets, conducting a cold search over as vast an area as the perimeter of the largest island in the South China Sea was another matter entirely. Bolan was no closer to unearthing Yang's whereabouts than when he'd first received word from Grimaldi and Kissinger that they'd blown up the Beechjet after determining that the runaway gangster was no longer aboard. Grimaldi had doubled back in the other F-14 to help with the search but he, too, had thusfar come up empty-handed.

Back at Stony Man Farm, the cybernetic team had lent what help it could, tapping into Satcam footage of the area during the likely time of Yang's aerial descent, but at no point had the Beechjet fallen under the gaze of the distant spy satellite. As he once more guided his jet over the jagged coastline, Smith summed up the predicament.

"You know, Colonel," he said, "if we knew where a needle was in a haystack, we could probably have it in our sights in no time flat and be able to thread it. But looking for it from scratch? No offense, sir, but I don't think it's gonna happen."

"I hear you, Lieutenant," Bolan responded through his headset. "And after this sweep we'll call it a night."

Bolan scanned the display screens before him. He knew

damn well he wasn't going to suddenly catch a glimpse of Jiang Yang running across some open stretch of beach. His hope was that after landing, the gangster would have ditched his parachute without bothering to gather it up and conceal it. Spotting the chute would be a starting point. Once they knew where Yang had touched down, they could send out an APB and dragnet the area with as much manpower as they could muster.

But Bolan knew that end of things would be problematic in itself, with Chinese officials dragging their feet in terms of helping with the search. In fact, formal complaints had already been lodged regarding the blowing up of Beechjet and the disruption of local flights by the two F-14s as they conducted a search through airspace normally used by no less than three different commercial airlines.

"Okay, Lieutenant," Bolan told the pilot, "it's a bust."

"Understood," Smith replied. "What next?"

The Executioner analyzed the situation. They could take the search to the ground, but he doubted they'd have any better luck. It made more sense to go with the premise that even though Yang had bailed from his plane, his ultimate destination most likely remained unchanged. Given that, the best course was to proceed to where Yang was bound and hope to catch up with him there.

"Let's move on," he told Smith. "To Hong Kong."

21

Hainan Island, China

Dawn was breaking when Jiang Yang was awakened from his guest quarters at Ki Dan's mansion and led by two guards through an early-morning mist to a private helipad to await the billionaire's arrival from the Philippines. On the ride from the casino a few hours earlier, it had been dark and the gangster had been too preoccupied with his own thoughts and the discomfort of his wet clothes to pay much heed to the paradise Dan had created for himself on this mountain bluff overlooking the thirty-six hole Emerald Cotillion Golf Course. As the mist began to fall away from the helipad like a parting curtain, Yang took his first good look at Ki Dan's coveted domain. He was awestruck.

Ki Dan had five separate residences scattered throughout the Pacific Rim, each one a high-priced testimony his expensive tastes and rampant ego, but Yang knew this was the property that the entrepreneur took the most pride in and called home.

Dan, a one-time fledgling architect, had designed the three-story, fifty-two-room main house himself, borrowing ideas and motifs from a range of sources. Yang would have had a hard time identifying which part of the house was inspired by I. M. Pei and which paid tribute to Frank Lloyd Wright.

All he knew for sure was that Dan had poured nearly ninety million dollars into the mansion, its landscaped grounds, Olympic-sized pool, polo field, and the trio of two-story guesthouses set on a gentle slope surrounded by a meandering botanical garden laced with man-made streams. All in all, it was as far a cry from the Jotuwi Port salvage yard as the gangster could have imagined.

I could get used to this, Yang thought as he fidgeted with the sash on the luxurious cashmere robe he wore over the black silk pajamas he'd been given at the mansion. The guards who brought Yang to the helipad directed him to an adjacent dining patio, where a maid and butler were meticulously laying out two place settings on a marble-topped table already filled with a number of silver serving dishes. The food was all covered, but Yang's stomach churned with anticipation as he detected the smell of bacon, fresh salmon, baked bread and coffee. He was about to ask if he could skip the formalities and start on breakfast when he heard the drone of an approaching helicopter.

As if one cue, a glint of sunlight streaked through the last remnants of mist and gleamed off the sides of a customized Bell 430 helicopter that had materialized out of the clouds overhead. A clear Plexiglas partition separated the patio area from the helipad, so Yang and the others were spared the brunt of the Bell's rotor wash as it set down. While the chopper didn't have the range of Hu Dzem's ill-fated Beechjet, Yang suspected the aircraft was every bit as well-appointed.

One of the guards slipped around the partition and opened the cabin door, then moved back, allowing Ki Dan to step down to the tarmac. Apparently the billionaire had slept on the plane, because he was attired, like Yang, in silk pajamas and a lounging robe. Dan's deep tan was every bit as real as Hu Dzem's was artificial, and the billionaire had made at least one plastic surgeon rich from the times he'd gone under the knife to dramatically alter his features so that he looked less like a Cantonese native than a WASP from the American heartland.

"Sorry to keep you waiting," Ki Dan said, offering Yang a gracious smile. "I came as soon as I could."

"I understand," Yang said.

Ki Dan engaged the Hong Kong gangster in more small talk as they took seats at the breakfast table and waited for the help to finish their preparations. Once the maid and butler had moved beyond earshot, however, the billionaire dropped all pretense and regarded Yang with a wary look.

"You're here because of what happened in Malaysia last night," Ki Dan stated. "Not a very pleasant turn of events."

Yang sipped his coffee, then forked a sliver of salmon onto a toast wedge, all the while fighting back the intimidation he'd felt since arriving at the helipad and seeing the fruits of Ki Dan's business labors. To get what he wanted he needed to show his would-be benefactor that he was void of desperation or want.

"I'm here because I decided to take you up on your offer," he said evenly. "I assume it's still on the table or you wouldn't be here."

Ki Dan chuckled faintly. "That offer was made before you managed to bungle a transaction involving one of my centrifuges."

"*Defective* centrifuge," Yang reminded Dan. "I took it off your hands for a fair price. What happened in Malaysia is no concern of yours."

Dan's surgically augmented eyelids narrowed but his smile remained pleasant, unthreatening. "I take it you erased any paper trail that could bring the authorities to my door."

The Hong Kong Dai Lo nodded. "If they bother looking, they'll see it as a triad deal gone wrong," he said. "Your hands are clean."

"We shall see."

Ki Dan busied himself with a slice of bacon, dipping it into his eggs, then chewing it with gusto. "So you want to come to work for me," he said, licking his fingertips.

"That was your offer," Yang said.

"Yes, it was. With a stipulation." A morning edition of the Hong Kong *Sentinel* had been placed on the table next to Dan's plate. He eyed it, then looked at Yang. "I take it if I turn to the obituaries I'll see Hu Dzem's name."

"It will be in tomorrow's paper. He dies this morning."

Ki Dan frowned. "The stipulation was that you would kill him. Did you happen to bring him along so I could see you do the honors?"

Yang shook his head. "You only said you wanted him dead. There was nothing about me attending to it personally."

"You're having someone else do your dirty work for you, is that it?"

"That's how it's done. As you well know." It was Yang's turn to smile.

Dan shrugged. "I suppose that's one less thing I'll have to teach you."

"We have a deal, then?"

"I have people in Hong Kong," the entrepreneur said. "Once I have word from them that Hu Dzem has indeed gone on to his ancestors, then, yes, we will have a deal. Until then, we will have to wait and see."

"Fair enough," Yang said. "You won't have long to wait."

"Good," Dan said. "Then let's enjoy the rest of our breakfast."

Yang sipped his juice, staring out at the South China Sea, which lay just beyond the golf course downhill from the estate. The waters were calm, glittering in the morning light like a trove of diamonds. Yang suspected that the Beechjet that had brought him to this rendezvous was by now resting in those same waters, no doubt brought down by his pursuers. He smiled as he imagined their reaction upon learning he had again outwitted them. They would continue to look for him, but once Hu Dzem was slain and Yang was firmly in Ki Dan's court, he knew that there was no way they would be able to get to him. The heat on him would cool off as it always did and he would move on with his new life, in a far better place than he'd been a few hours ago.

There was one curious matter about the offer Yang had received to join forces with Ki Dan. The gangster took advantage of a lull in the conversation to broach the subject. With as much nonchalance as he could muster, he said to Ki Dan, "You never mentioned why you wanted Hu Dzem killed."

"You're right," Dan replied. "I didn't."

"That's it?"

Ki Dan put down his fork, then dabbed his lips with an ironed napkin bearing his initials. "Let's just say Hu Dzem and I have a history."

Yang was still curious to know more but felt it was best to leave well enough alone. "Well," he said, "soon it will be ancient history."

22

Hong Kong

Li Chuannan awoke groggily to the bleeping of his alarm clock. The sun had just come up and light was straining through the closed shade of his bedroom. Chuannan wasn't a day person. If anything, dawn was usually when he went to bed after a night's carousing. This morning, however, thanks to his cryptic conversation with Jiang Yang, he had different plans. Plotting the details had encroached on his sleep, but Chuannan figured it had been time well-spent. There was little margin for error in what he was about to do, and it was important that he had everything worked out.

Chuannan's suite was one floor down from Hu Dzem's penthouse office at the Dynasty Club. The place was sparsely furnished, and the gangster's refrigerator was equally barren. He downed what was left of a quart of milk and called it breakfast, then stopped by the bathroom long enough to give himself his daily steroid injection. Then, he quickly dressed so he could turn his focus to the task at hand.

Chuannan had a four-gun arsenal stashed in the top drawer of his dresser. In addition to his freshly cleaned Tokarev TT-33, he had a Bulldog .44 Special that proved far more imposing out on the streets when he was doing shakedowns for Hu Dzem's loan sharks and extortionists. And on those occasions when he knew he was in for an all-out firefight, there was a 30-round Ingram M-10, less than a foot long with its wire stock collapsed but still capable of a wallop matching guns twice its size.

This day, however, Chuannan was most concerned with the least impressive weapon in his possession, an antiquated, 2-shot .41 caliber derringer that, even with its built-in silencer, was half the size of his compact Tokarev. The popgun had no prints on it, and Chuannan intended to keep it that way. He picked up the derringer with a silk handkerchief and slipped it into his pocket on his way out the door.

Chuannan took the elevator up to Hu Dzem's deserted office. The chairman and his ever-present bodyguards wouldn't be in for another hour. The bouncer shut off the controls to one of the surveillance cameras, knowing he'd have ample time to return and switch it back on before Dzem returned. He then took the stairs down two flights to the hallway lined with rooms used by the Dynasty's prostitutes. He stopped at one of the doors and rapped lightly on the frame. When no one answered, he fished through his pockets for the master key. He was about to unlock the door when the latch turned. Eva Kelmin opened the door a crack and peered tiredly past the safety chain at Chuannan.

"Let me in," the one-time wrestler told her.

"It's early."

"Let me in," Chuannan repeated firmly.

Eva trembled, stammering, "I didn't do anything wrong."

"No one said you did," the gangster responded. "I have a proposition for you."

Eva warily let Chuannan in. "What's this about?" she asked.

Chuannan got to the point. "How would you like to earn your freedom?" he asked.

"My freedom?"

"You heard me," Chuannan said. "How would you like to walk out of here today and be done with this?"

Eva stared at Chuannan. "I don't understand."

"What's to understand?" Chuannan countered. "I'm offering you an out. Do you want it or not?"

"Of course I want to get out of here," Eva said. "But there's no way you're just going to let me go. I know you better than that."

"There is one small catch," Chuannan confessed.

"What is it?"

When Chuannan reached into his pocket, Eva cringed and took an involuntary step back.

"Relax," Chuannan told her. He held out what at first appeared to be nothing more than a wadded handkerchief. When Chuannan folded back the layers of silk, however, she found herself staring at the derringer.

"Do you know how to use one of these?" Chuannan asked. "If not I can show you."

Eva bypassed the question and asked, "What do you want me to do with it?"

"I'm going to hide it behind the planter near the wet bar in Hu Dzem's office," Chuannan told her. "Later this morning you're to go up there and tell Hu Dzem you want to see him privately. When you get him alone, you're going to seduce him."

"Seduce him? How?"

Chuannan smiled. "With all the practice you've had, I'm sure you can figure a way."

"I still don't understand," Eva said.

"It's simple," the gangster told her. "You get Hu Dzem to send out his bodyguards, then you get him in a compromising position any way you know how. The more depraved, the better."

"Why?"

"You're asking too many questions," Chuannan told her. "Just do what I say and you will earn your freedom."

"You haven't said what you want done with the gun."

"That part's simple, too," Chuannan said. "Once you've

compromised Dzem, you're going to bait him into playing rough. When that happens, you'll take the gun and kill him."

WHILE LI CHUANNAN was conspiring with Eva Kelmin, Hu Dzem was three blocks away, starting his day as he'd started nearly every day over the past dozen years—with some before-hours pampering at the Micau Acupressure Clinic. It was one of the few enterprises owned by the triad chairman that operated with total legality. Dzem owned a few dozen other clinics and massage parlors that were fronts for prostitution, but Micau was staffed solely by licensed professionals and was actually known as one of the better acupressure facilities in all of Hong Kong.

Lying facedown on his favorite massage table, towel draped discreetly across his ample buttocks, Hu Dzem tried to think peaceful thoughts as Rei Lan, the Micau's thin, elegant-looking sixty-year-old proprietor, ran her expert fingers across his shoulders, slowly loosening knots of tension that lay beneath folds of the man's orangish skin.

"Always the same place," she said softly.

"Always the same problems," Hu Dzem murmured. "I'm getting too old for all this."

"Ten years I've been hearing you say that," Rei Lan said.

"This time I mean it," Hu Dzem said.

"Of course," the woman said with a knowing smile. "Shh. You're getting tense all over again."

Hu Dzem tried to free his mind of trying concerns, but he continued to be haunted by the sense that last night's news from Malaysia would mark a turning point with the triad, one that would work against him. He'd gone to bed convinced that Jiang Yang's failed attempt to broker the nuclear centrifuges would ultimately work in his favor. But when he'd awoken this morning and talked to a few of his most trusted confidants, he'd learned that many of his rivals within San Hop Kwan were saying that if he'd been more cooperative with

Yang's venture, it might have succeeded. Dzem found the notion preposterous. How could anyone make him out to be a scapegoat for what had happened? It made no sense. And yet, there it was. Like it or not, on top of all the other problems that came with trying to run his organization, he had to contend with the notion that his view of things was obsolete. Such disrespect! he thought. What was this world coming to?

Rei Lan was about to chide Hu Dzem for tensing up on her again when the door suddenly swung open. In strode one of the chairman's bodyguards, followed by a uniformed police officer in his early thirties with thin lips and a furrowed brow.

"There is nothing illegal going on here!" Rei Lan snapped at the officer. "You have no business here!"

Hu Dzem glanced up at the officer and sighed. The man, Shu Ter-Ci, was a corrupt cop who made more money under the table stooging for the triads than he did as a ten-year veteran of the Hong Kong police force. "It's all right," Dzem told the woman. "Just give us a moment."

Rei Lan relaxed visibly and handed Hu Dzem a bathrobe, then headed out of the room, pausing before the policeman long enough to scold him. "You could at least knock next time."

"Of course," Shu Ter-Ci responded politely. "Forgive me."

Appeased, the woman followed the bodyguard out of the room, closing the door behind her. Hu Dzem slipped into the bathrobe and stepped down from the massage table.

"I guess I will have to change my routine so I'm less easy to track down this early in the morning," he told the officer.

"I apologize," Ter-Ci replied. "But I have some information you should know about before you go to the Dynasty. In fact, you may want to avoid going there altogether."

"What now?" Dzem demanded.

"We rousted a transient for burglary a few hours ago," the police officer reported. "He wanted to cut some kind of deal to avoid charges, so we put him into interrogation to see if he had any useful information. He mentioned something regarding one of your girls at the Dynasty. One of the Americans."

Ter-Ci proceeded to describe how the transient had seen Eva Kelmin ushered into the brothel a week ago, then subsequently relayed the incident to a man and woman prowling around the hotel the day before looking for a woman matching Eva's description.

As he listened, Hu Dzem felt a sinking feeling in his chest.

"Between you and me," the officer went on, "I know there are other agencies on the lookout for this girl on behalf of her father in America. If they found out that she is being held at the Dynasty—"

Ter-Ci didn't need to finish his sentence. Hu Dzem nodded, realizing the implications. Here he was, angry at the thought Jiang Yang might bring the authorities sniffing around triad business with his nuke dealing, and now his own penchant for young American girls had apparently stirred up the same problem, heaping more grief onto his already overloaded plate. And, pressing as his concerns about the upcoming triad elections were, he knew this new problem would have to take precedence.

"Did this transient give you a description of the people he spoke to?" he asked the rogue cop.

Shu Ter-Ci nodded and handed Hu Dzem police sketches of the man and woman in question.

Neither of them looked familiar, but the chairman had a feeling that might soon change.

"If they are planning some sort of raid, you don't want to be caught up in it," the officer advised. "You might want to think about moving this woman to another location as well."

Hu Dzem glared at the man. "I'm capable of figuring how best to deal with this matter."

Ter-Ci took a step back. "Of course."

Hu Dzem waved the man off and started to change into his clothes. Moments after the officer had left, Rei Lan returned.

"We didn't finish your session," she said.

"Another time," Hu Dzem said gruffly.

The chairman took the composite sketches of Christine Wood and Terrance Molvico and stormed into the hallway.

"Get in touch with my best field men," he told his bodyguards. "Have them drop whatever they're doing and get in touch with me. We have a situation."

23

When he was on assignment, Mack Bolan rarely got much sleep, so he'd learned to make the best of it. Within a half hour of reaching Hong Kong, he'd beelined to the hotel Barbara Price had lined up for the Stony Man team and had dropped into a deep slumber. Four hours later, he was up, refreshed and ready for what he was sure would be another grueling day. Jack Grimaldi and John Kissinger had already gone out for breakfast and were in the dining area of the two bedroom suite, scanning maps and the screen of Bolan's computer as they plotted how to run with the latest leads fed to them from the cyberteam back in Virginia.

"Pull up a chair," Kissinger told Bolan, gesturing to a takeout bag on the table. "We brought you some food."

Bolan sat down and raided the bag, coming up with a bagel, protein bar and two oranges. There was a cup of coffee as well, still warm. "What do we have?" he asked as he clawed the rind off one of the oranges.

"Bad news first," Grimaldi said. "Yang's still at large. No trace of him here, and the teams scouring Hainan Island have come up with squat so far."

"That doesn't leave much room for good news," Bolan said.

"Afraid not," Kissinger stated. "The best we have to go on is a list of the guy's favorite haunts here in Hong Kong."

"That's a start," Bolan said.

Kissinger moved the map across the table so both he and

Bolan could see it. He pointed out locations as he briefed the Executioner. "We're just a few blocks from his apartment. He's got a three-room place twenty floors up a high-rise near the main drag. I already tried the phone. Zip."

"Not likely he's going to show there," Bolan guessed. "Where else?"

"His business front is an office suite in some strip mall near the harbor," Kissinger went on. "Recorded message says they open shop at ten."

Bolan glanced at his watch. It was a little past nine.

"Door number three's just off the tenderloin strip on Hennessey Avenue," Kissinger said. "There's a brothel there run by Yang's boss. Yang's probably not in the mood to get called on the carpet, but maybe he figures he doesn't have a choice."

"Brothel, huh?" Bolan said.

Grimaldi interjected, "Barb tells me you already know about Inter-Trieve running that angle on a missing persons case."

Bolan nodded, finishing off the orange. "Yeah," he said. "Glorified bountyhunters, right?"

"Right," Grimaldi reported. "I've already been on the horn with one of their desk jockeys and it looks like a couple of their agents have the place under surveillance. If you want, I've got a contact number."

"In a minute," Bolan said. "Any other leads?"

"Yeah, but they're all long shots," Kissinger reported. "I think we're better off sticking with these three."

Bolan nodded as he took a bite from his bagel and washed it down with coffee. "I say we defer to Inter-Trieve for the time being and try the office," he said. "If we head out now, we can probably intercept whoever shows up first for work."

"Works for me," Kissinger said.

"Ditto," Grimaldi added.

"Let's do it, then," Bolan said, rising from the table.

Grimaldi waved a slip of paper. "You want that number?"

Bolan mulled it over a moment, then said, "Have Barb give them a heads-up on our plan."

"NOTHING GOING ON THERE yet," Wood said, lowering the binoculars she'd borrowed from Sam Chen. Chen was standing beside her, wearing headphones as he hooked a four-inch monitor up to a portable transceiver unit on a table near the window overlooking Hennessey Avenue and the Dynasty Club. Behind them Terrance Molvico was rigging himself with the wire he'd be wearing when he crossed the street in hopes of finding out whether or not Eva Kelmin was in one of the brothel rooms.

"Well, it shouldn't be too long," Molvico said. "I'm sure the horn dogs start rolling in sometime after breakfast. First sign of activity, we'll go for it."

Chen glanced back at Molvico and gave a thumbs-up. "Coming through loud and clear," he said. "Let's check the minicam."

Wood set the binoculars aside and grabbed a pair of thick-framed horn-rimmed glasses lying on the table next to Chen's transceiver. The high-tech spy camera was imbedded in the bridgework, with the frames serving as antennas.

"Here you go, hubby," she said, placing the glasses on Molvico's nose. "Now you've definitely got the Horny Geek look down pat."

Molvico stared at the monitor. Once Chen had secured the feed, the screen brightened with an image of itself, transmitting Molvico's cam-view with sharp clarity.

"Decent," Molvico said. He turned and stared at Wood's chest. "Only thing missing is the X-ray vision."

Wood punched Molvico on the shoulder. "Pervert."

"Hey, just trying to stay in character," he protested. He finished buttoning his shirt, then slipped a SIG-Sauer P-226 behind his back and tightened his belt to make sure the gun would stay put inside his waistband. A thick woolen sport coat was draped over the chair beside him. As he put it on, he asked Chen, "How about if I go for a stroll so we can check the range on my mike?"

"Good idea," Chen said, fingering his mustache as he double-checked the controls on his transceiver. "We'll do the same with your hearing aid."

Molvico nodded, tapping the flesh-colored minireceiver tucked inside his right ear. The apparatus, partially concealed by the operative's hair, was designed to look like a conventional hearing aid but served as a radio link to the transceiver.

"As long as we're doing the makeover thing," Wood said, "I'm gonna go get my sunglasses and pull back my hair."

"While you're at it, how about double-checking on our backup?" Chen suggested.

"Will do," she said. "Ring me once we're ready and I'll get the car."

Chen reminded Wood, "Just don't hit the alley until we're sure Terry's got the girl and is headed for the fire escape."

"Got it," Wood said.

She turned to Molvico. "And you don't make your move until we've got the lane blocked so we can shoot out of there and get a head start for the airport."

"No problemo," Molvico said.

"That's it, then," Chen said. "Let's do it."

Chen sat down before the transceiver as Molvico led Wood out into the hallway.

"Remember," Molvico told her, "if Eva's not there I'll do the cold feet thing and meet you back here."

"Look who's raining on the parade now," Wood teased.

"You're right," Molvico said. "I take it back."

"Now, go," she told him. "Break a leg."

Molvico headed for the elevator as Wood let herself into her room and called Inter-Trieve's Hong Kong office on her cell. While she was waiting for an answer she pulled her hair back and put on her sunglasses, then eyed herself in the mirror. She hadn't bothered with any makeup, figuring the more nondescript she looked, the better.

"Yuck," she said to her reflection.

Once somebody picked up, Wood quickly confirmed that three backup agents would have a utility van parked in front of the Dynasty by the time the plan was put into action. Once they had word that Molvico was headed for the fire escape with Eva, they'd pull out and block the right lane just shy of the alleyway, giving Wood a clear getaway route. The office dispatcher was telling her whereabouts at the airport their plane would be waiting for them when Wood's call waiting signal bleeped. She quickly signed off with the dispatcher then took the other call.

24

"This won't be easy," Bolan said as he pulled to a stop across the street from the strip mall housing the office space rented out to Jiang Yang. The mall, located on a wedge of land between a wooded park and one of the marinas servicing Victoria Harbour, was a U-shaped complex, two stories high, wrapped around an open courtyard filled with tables, all of which were occupied by patrons of the ground floor coffee and pastry shops. Given that Yang's Pacific Rim Tourist Industries address was 113-A, it seemed a fair bet the offices were located on the lower floor. And therein lay the problem.

"One wrong move and we've got bullets flying through a crowd of innocent bystanders," Grimaldi said, voicing Bolan's concern.

Grimaldi was in the backseat of their rental Chevy Cavalier. Kissinger was up front riding next to Bolan, holding the foldout map he'd used to give directions. He checked his watch, then told the others, "It's still a few minutes before ten. If we're here ahead of Yang's people, we might be able to intercept them around back in the parking lot. I know it's probably crowded there, too, but—"

"Hang on," Bolan interjected. He'd been gazing into the courtyard, searching the faces of those out breakfasting at the tables. One of the faces was familiar. "Second table in on your right," he said. "Right next to the fountain. Guy with the crew cut and mustache. Long sleeved polo shirt."

"Gotcha," Grimaldi said, pinpointing the man in question. "What about him?"

"Akira e-mailed me some mug shots of the crew Yang ran with," Bolan explained. "This guy matches up. I don't remember his name, but he's supposed to be a numbers guy."

"Right guy to have running a business front," Grimaldi said.

"That'd be my guess," Bolan replied. "Yang probably left him to run things while he took another crew down to Malaysia."

"Makes sense," Kissinger said. Noting the woman seated across from the man in question, he added, "If you're right, my money says the lady's part of the mix."

"Looks like they're shooting the breeze before they open up," Grimaldi said. "And unless she plans on wolfing down that Danish in one bite, they're gonna be there awhile."

"If that's the case, we might as well put it to our advantage," Bolan said, sizing up the situation. "Cowboy, why don't you circle around back and find the rear entrance to the office? Odds are it'll be locked, but if we can make sure these two stay put long enough, you can—"

"Just a sec," Kissinger interrupted, eyes on the courtyard.

Bolan glanced back and saw the man with the crew cut rise from the table, plugging one ear as he fielded a cell phone call with the other. After exchanging a few words, the man nodded and slipped the phone in his pocket. He said something to the woman at the table, then took his coffee and started down the walkway leading from the courtyard to the street. The woman, meanwhile, grabbed her pastry and fished through her pocket for a set of keys as she rose to her feet.

"I think we better move on to Plan B," Grimaldi said. Seeing the man with the crew cut circle around a tan Porsche Targa parked along the curb across from them, he quickly added, "Three on one. How about we button him down?"

Bolan shook his head. "Let me follow him," he said. "If that was Yang he was talking to, maybe he'll lead me to him."

"Worth a shot," Kissinger replied, reaching for the door handle. "That would leave the lady for us."

"Yeah, but play it safe," Bolan cautioned. "There's no guarantee she'll be running the shop alone."

"Got it."

By the time Grimaldi and Kissinger had stepped out of the Chevy, the man with the crew cut had his Porsche in gear and was pulling out into traffic. From the sidewalk, Grimaldi watched Bolan throw the Chevy into reverse and back into the alleyway behind him, then pull out into the street. A couple of cars had already fallen in behind the Porsche, but Bolan was in a good position to tail his mark.

"Let's just hope it doesn't come down to a high-speed chase," Grimaldi told Kissinger. "Otherwise I like the Porsche's chances."

"Not our problem in any event," Kissinger said, eyes on the woman with the Danish. She was weaving through the other diners in the courtyard, making her way to one of the shopfronts. "Let's get cracking."

Grimaldi and Kissinger headed into the courtyard, walking as fast as they could without drawing undue attention. They caught up with the woman just as she was letting herself into the office suite. By the time she noticed them, Kissinger was already pushing his way past her, withdrawing his Colt pistol from its web holster. Grimaldi, meanwhile, discreetly took hold of the woman's arm, cutting her off before she could speak.

"Let's keep it quiet, okay?" he said, assuming, correctly, that she could speak English. "Don't make a scene."

A flash of fear crept across the woman's face as Grimaldi guided her inside and closed the door behind them. She dropped her Danish onto the carpeted floor as she tried to free herself from the hold Grimaldi had on her.

"We don't have any money here," she said.

"No problem," Grimaldi assured her. "This isn't a robbery. We're looking for information."

"Not to mention your boss," Kissinger said. He'd already scanned the room and circled around the service counter. With due caution, he placed himself next to a doorway leading to the back room, gun in hand, then called out, "Anyone back there?"

"There's no one else here," the woman told him.

Kissinger waited a moment, then checked for himself. The back room was empty save for stacks of file boxes and a table with a coffee machine and fax machine set next to a desk and swivel chair. He returned to the office, shaking his head at Grimaldi, who had guided the woman into a chair near the service counter. As Kissinger began to methodically search the office, Grimaldi moved past a spindle rack filled with brochures and closed the blinds, then retrieved the pastry from the floor and handed it to the woman.

"Where's Yang?" he asked her.

"I don't know," the woman responded. She tossed the Danish in a nearby wastebasket.

"Your friend," Grimaldi prompted. "The one you were having breakfast with. Was he talking to Yang?"

"I don't know," the woman said.

"Wrong answer," Grimaldi said. "He was in a hurry to go somewhere. Where to?"

"Who are you?" the woman snapped back. "What gives you the right to interrogate me like this?"

"We're the good guys," Grimaldi informed her. "You work for criminals. That means we get to ask questions, all right? And if you get smart and start answering them, maybe we'll get the idea you're not in it with them. Maybe we'll get the idea you're just a hardworking woman trying to earn a living with no idea she was being used by said criminals. Do we understand each other?"

"You want to cut a deal," the woman said.

"There you go," Grimaldi said, smiling faintly. "I knew you could figure it out."

"I would help you if I could," the woman said, "but I've only been here two weeks. I answer a phone that rings maybe twice a day, I pass out travel brochures to anyone who comes in the door, and I make coffee when somebody asks me to."

"Sounds like a pretty nice job," Grimaldi said. "Did it ever occur to you it was maybe a little too easy?"

"When I was hired they told me not to ask questions," the woman said stiffly. "So I don't."

"Then I'll ask them for you," Grimaldi said. "Do you know what a front is? A money-laundering operation?"

"I don't do anything illegal," the woman insisted. "And I haven't seen anything illegal go on around me."

Grimaldi continued to question the woman but got nowhere. Kissinger wasn't having much better luck. The front office was clean, supplied with nothing other than generic tourist information and a few files filled with innocuous paperwork. When he double-checked the back room, however, one of the desk drawers was locked. When he came back to the main room and asked the woman for a key, she shook her head.

"That's Mr. Yang's desk," she said. "He's the only one with a key that I know of."

Kissinger reached into his back pocket, pulling out a set of lock picks. "Not anymore," he told the woman.

It took him all of thirty seconds to spring the desk lock. Inside the drawer he found a few sheets of paper clipped together. He skimmed the contents as he brought the papers back to Grimaldi.

"What have you got?" Grimaldi asked.

"Centrifuge schematics," Kissinger said. "Phone number scribbled in the margins. I'm not on top of international area codes, but my guess is if we dial this number, we get Indonesia."

"The Aceh rebels," Grimaldi said.

Kissinger nodded. "Exhibit A for The People versus Jiang Yang. Now we just have to find the bastard."

JIANG YANG PACED the guest room where he'd just placed his cell phone call to Ling Thieu, the San Hop Kwan colleague who ran things at his office front near Victoria Harbour. Wary that Li Chuannan might not be able to pull off Hu Dzem's execution, Yang had asked Thieu to go to the Dynasty and check on things. If Chuannan had faltered, Thieu was to see to it that the chairman wound up dead, preferably by noon. Between the two thugs, Yang figured the job would be done, but he was still nagged by feelings of uncertainty.

With so much at stake, Yang wished he was in a position to see to matters personally. He would have liked to see the look on Hu Dzem's face when he pulled the trigger. But, given the circumstances, Yang would have to be content to have the execution carried out by surrogates.

"Get it done," he stated aloud, staring out the window overlooking the southernmost edge of Ki Dan's estate. A brick wall rose from the edge of the bluff, beyond which lay the steep drop to the golf course. An observation deck extended out over the wall, affording a panoramic view of the sea. Yang tried to think a few days ahead, to when Hu Dzem was out of the way and he was firmly in Ki Dan's court. Maybe a few days from now he'd be out on that observation deck, smoking cigars with the billionaire as they watched the sun set and planned their next bit of intrigue. Ki Dan probably had a bevy of high-priced call girls at his beck and call, and after the sun was down the two of them would come back here and indulge themselves. Yang would have his pick of any kind of woman he wanted. Life would be sweet.

For any of Yang's fantasies to come true, his underlings would have to come through for him. His fate was in their hands, and when Yang's gaze strayed from the view and fell back on the wall clock in his room, he was beset all over again with worrisome doubts.

Again he muttered, "Get it done."

FOR SEVERAL BLOCKS, Bolan was able to maintain visual contact with the Porsche, all the while keeping several cars between them. The deeper they headed into the heart of the city, however, the more congested the traffic became, not only with cars but also trucks and other large vehicles that obstructed Bolan's view, making it more difficult to stay on the other car's tail.

Halfway through the garment district, the Porsche zipped around a Volkswagen minibus to make a last-second lane change. Bolan, boxed in on either side, was unable to match the maneuver. He was concerned about losing ground on the other man, and his fears were borne out soon after when the Porsche driver goosed his accelerator to race a red light. Bolan, five cars back, had no choice but to stop.

The Executioner cursed his luck. He had no reason to believe the other man knew he was being followed, but it didn't matter. When the light changed, he did his best to wrangle through the snarling traffic, but even after he'd regained some of the ground he'd lost, the Porsche was nowhere to be seen.

When he stopped for the next light, Bolan let out a long breath, fighting his frustration. The street signs were printed in English as well as Chinese, and once he figured out where he was, Bolan grabbed the foldout map Kissinger had left on the passenger seat. He pinpointed the intersection on the map, checked the surrounding area and the Executioner's spirits rallied.

"So that's where you're headed," he whispered.

25

Just as Li Chuannan was the brawn Hu Dzem turned to when he needed brute force, Hung and Xiao Deng were the brains, men the chairman could rely on to carry out assignments requiring a measure of finesse and insight. Twin brothers in their early thirties, the Dengs had been recruited away from a Hong Kong think tank by a cousin who'd convinced them their talents could carry them far within the ranks of San Hop Kwan. They'd started out doing research and investigative work for Hu Dzem, helping the chairman determine high-yield extortion targets and plotting more efficient ways to run the number rackets. From there, they'd graduated to surveillance assignments, compiling dossiers on wayward police officers and public figures whose indiscretions made them vulnerable to bribes and blackmail, thereby bolstering the triad's network of moles and informants within the Hong Kong government and police department. Their work in the field required that the twins become proficient with firearms. In time, they were supplementing their detective work with occasional contract hits, taking out people deemed harder targets than the lowlifes usually turned over to goons like Li Chuannan.

When summoned by Hu Dzem and told of a possible raid on the Dynasty, the Dengs had fallen back on their expertise and quickly deduced the most likely staging area for the raid.

Just as quickly, they'd figured out a course of action for dealing with the problem. Less than ten minutes after that, the twins strolled into the White Orchid Inn and made their way to the front desk. Once the clerk had finished registering a couple of guests, they were ready to make their move.

The clerk, a woman in her twenties, made a lame joke about seeing double, then asked the twins, "Do you have reservations?"

"We're looking for some people," Hung Deng told the woman, presenting the composite sketches of Christine Wood and Terrance Molvico. "We have reason to believe they're staying here."

The clerk eyed the sketches noncommittally, then asked, "What is this regarding?"

"A personal matter," Xiao said.

"I'm sorry, but we have a policy regarding the privacy of our guests," the woman replied.

Hung Deng smiled graciously. "Forgive me," he said. "I suppose we should have shown you our credentials up front."

"Are you with the police?" the woman asked.

Hung shook his head and pretended to check his watch, in the process letting the sleeve of his sport coat ride up his arm. Then he nonchalantly raised his hand to his face, idly stroking his chin, in the process giving the clerk a good, long look at the San Hop Kwan dragon tattooed on his wrist. The woman paled visibly. Xiao reached out and tapped the composite sketches, letting the clerk see his tattoo as well. With his other hand, he unbuttoned his coat and let it flop open enough to expose the butt of a Walther P-22 nestled in its web holster.

"We want their room numbers," Xiao explained calmly. "And keys."

Hu Dzem smiled faintly as he received the news over his cell phone.

"If you can wring some information out of them, fine," he told Xiao Deng once the twin confirmed that the man and woman who'd been sniffing around for Eva Kelmin were staying at the White Orchid Inn. "But if they resist, do what you have to."

"Understood," Xiao responded.

"Report to me once you have results," the chairman said, staring out the tinted windows of the armor-plated Lincoln Town Car carrying him down a back street to the rear entrance of the Dynasty Club. One of his bodyguards was behind the wheel. The other sat beside him in the backseat, vigilantly casing out the littered passageway for signs of suspicious activity. "I'll be in my office."

"Are you sure that's a wise idea?" Xiao asked.

"No one's going to keep me from going about my business," Hu Dzem responded. "You do your job and let me take care of mine."

"Understood," Xiao repeated.

Hu Dzem slipped the cell phone back in his pocket. They were coming up on the Dynasty's rear parking lot when a police squad car rolled into view in the alley. Hu Dzem's driver slowed down. The bodyguard in the backseat slid his hand inside his coat, reaching for his pistol.

"It's all right," Hu Dzem assured his men. "He's with us."

The bodyguards relaxed, recognizing the man in the squad car as the same rogue cop they'd encountered earlier at the acupressure clinic. Hu Dzem had arranged for Shu Ter-Ci to come by the Dynasty to provide backup. If the officer had followed orders, by now there were also a handful of undercover cops roaming Hennessey Avenue and the alleyways surrounding the hotel. Anyone showing up at the Dynasty this morning with the idea of freeing Eva Kelmin was going to be in for a rude surprise.

TERRANCE MOLVICO WAS loitering in front of a news kiosk just up the street from the Dynasty Club when Sam Chen's voice crackled in his earbud transceiver.

"You're transmitting loud and clear," Chen told him. "What's more, it looks like somebody's just gone into the Dynasty looking for some action."

"That would make it showtime for me," Molvico muttered, moving away from the kiosk. "I'm on my way."

"I'll wait until you're in, then I'll have Christine get the car," Chen said.

"Sounds like a plan," Molvico said, veering his way through the heavy pedestrian traffic on Hennessey Avenue. "What about backup?"

Chen reported, "They're pulling up as we speak."

Molvico glanced down the block and saw a nondescript panel truck backing into a parking spot in front of the Dynasty Club. As he drew closer, he recognized the man behind the wheel as Mitch Carlisle, a fellow Inter-Trieve agent with the Hong Kong office. Molvico passed the truck, then drew in a breath and detoured to the entryway leading into the Dynasty.

"Here goes," he told himself.

Throwing the door open, Molvico swaggered into the reception area, doing his best to look like a tourist eager to lighten his money belt in exchange for some quality time with a woman who could take his mind off his problems. An attractive middle-aged woman was standing near a set of elevators, talking to the client Sam Chen had mentioned.

"You'll get off on the second floor and one of our men will see to it that you're taken care of," the woman told the man.

Before the woman could turn to him, Molvico was distracted by the opening of another set of doors leading into the reception area from the back parking lot. Suddenly, Molvico found himself staring at the Dynasty's proprietor, Hu Dzem.

The chairman met Molvico's gaze with an intent look, then slowly allowed a thin smile to crease his face.

"Welcome to the Dynasty," Hu Dzem told Molvico. "Let's see if we can take care of you."

LI CHUANNAN WAS distracted as he escorted the Dynasty's first client of the day down the second-floor hallway. Hu Dzem would arrive any minute and the enforcer's mind was more focused on the plan he would soon be carrying out than seeing to the needs of the middle-aged Cantonese retailer who'd just shelled out the equivalent of two hundred dollars U.S. for a half-hour session with one of the inner room girls.

"So, am I?" the retailer asked, irritation in his voice. Chuannan snapped out of his reverie and turned to the man.

"Are you what?"

"Am I going to be able to pick a girl out of a lineup?"

"You're too early for that," Chuannan told the man brusquely. "We have only two girls who do spanking. But, yes, you can choose whichever one of them you want."

"Only two?"

"This is the Dynasty," Chuannan told the man, "Trust me, you'll have trouble enough deciding between just two."

The hostess had already called upstairs from the reception area, and the two young women in question had dutifully positioned themselves outside their respective rooms. One was a black-haired Hong Kong native in her early twenties, wearing a white teddy that complimented her voluptuous figure. The other woman was a fair-skinned Russian several years older, on the thin side with red hair and dazzling blue eyes. She was dressed in a see-through lace slip with matching gartered stockings. Both greeted the retailer with well-practiced come-hither smiles.

"You're right," the retailer said. He ran his tongue across his upper lip as he ogled the women. "How much for both?"

"We normally don't allow that," the bouncer said, "but if you want to pay double, I'll clear things downstairs."

"Done." The retailer fished through his wallet and counted out a few bills, then turned them over to Chuannan, who fisted the money and slipped it into his pocket. The woman overheard the exchange. They quickly conferred with each other, deciding to use the Russian's room. Still smiling, they took the man by the hand and led him into the room. The Russian winked at Chuannan before closing the door.

Chuannan sighed and doubled back toward the elevators, stopping at Eva Kelmin's room. She opened the door seconds after he knocked. She was wearing what Chuannan had told her was Hu Dzem's favorite outfit, a skintight, sleeveless black leather dress with a plunging neckline and slit skirt, topped off with knee-high boots. Her nerves were on edge, and it showed in her features.

"Are you ready?" Chuannan asked her.

"As ready as I'll ever be," she said, her voice trembling.

"Just do what I told you and everything will be fine," he assured her. "Hu Dzem should be here any minute. I'll set things up, then give you the call to come see him."

"What about the bodyguards?" Eva asked. "Even if I get them out of the room, they're going to hear the gun."

"The gun has a built-in silencer," Chuannan told her. "Not that it matters. They aren't going to hear a thing."

"You're going to kill them?"

Chuannan stared hard at Eva. "What do you think?"

Eva nodded, biting her lower lip.

"Pull yourself together," Chuannan warned her. "If Hu Dzem suspects anything, you can kiss your freedom goodbye."

Chuannan left Eva to deal with her anxiety. He took the elevator to the ground floor, then stepped out into the reception area, which was normally the province of the Dynasty's hostess, Dee Wong, an attractive middle-aged woman who'd ingratiated herself to Hu Dzem during her years as a prostitute.

Wong was nowhere to be seen. Instead, Hu Dzem was personally attending to an American client who'd shown up while Chuannan was contending with the retailer. The man wore a bulky sport coat and thick-rimmed eyeglasses.

"If you could arrange that, excellent," the American was telling Hu Dzem.

"Give me just a moment," Hu Dzem told the client.

Dee Wong emerged from a back room with one of Hu Dzem's bodyguards. The other guard was standing near the elevator. When he exchanged a glance with Chuannan, the enforcer cringed inwardly. It wasn't just the cold expression in the man's eyes that sent a wave of paranoia racing through Chuannan. There was also the matter of Hu Dzem dealing with a client personally, something he'd never done before. Something was amiss.

"Have a seat," Dee Wong told the American, gesturing at one of the plush velvet chairs spaced along the paneled walls of the reception area. "I'll bring you some tea while you're waiting."

"That'd be fine," the man said. "If you want to slip in something a little stronger while you're at it, even better."

"I'll see what I can do," the woman told him.

One of the bodyguards stayed behind while the other led Hu Dzem into the elevator. The chairman gestured for Chuannan to come with them. Chuannan obliged, doing his best to ignore the rivulet of cold sweat that suddenly dripped down his spine.

Had they found out? he wondered. Had he turned off the wrong surveillance camera this morning? Had somebody witnessed him plotting with Eva?

He casually unfastened the button to his sport coat, not so much for ventilation as to put his gun within easier reach. If they were on to him, his well-laid plan was out the window and he would have to improvise, perhaps to the extent of trying to kill Hu Dzem in the elevator.

Once the doors had hissed closed and the elevator had begun to groan upward, Chuannan decided to force the issue.

"Eva says she needs to see you this morning," he said. "As soon as possible. She says it's important."

Hu Dzem made a guttural noise and muttered under his breath, "What, she's in on it, too?"

Chuannan turned slightly, concealing his hand as it closed around the butt of his Tokarev TT-33. He held back from pulling the gun out, however, when he saw that neither Hu Dzem nor the bodyguard were making a move for their weapons.

"In on what?" Chuannan asked, a slight rasp in his voice.

"We have a problem," Hu Dzem said. "It concerns the man downstairs."

Chuannan relaxed his grip on the pistol and exhaled. The elevator came to a stop on the top floor. The men stepped out and started down the hall to the penthouse office.

"Our *client* downstairs works for some agency trying to get their hands on the Kelmin girl," Hu Dzem told Chuannan. "We obviously aren't about to let that happen."

"What do we do?" Chuannan asked, his mind still racing, trying figure how this twist of events would impact on his plans.

"He asked to see all our white girls," Hu Dzem explained. "I told him we'd arrange a lineup. I want you to go back down and say you'll escort him up so that he can have his pick. Once you have him on the elevator, stop between floors and work him over. Just enough to soften him up." Hu Dzem stopped before the door to his office, then looked at Chuannan. "When you're done, bring him here to me so we can find out what he knows."

Chuannan nodded, his stomach knotting. Too much was happening too fast. He wasn't sure what his next move should be. Hu Dzem saw the hesitation in his eyes and frowned.

"What's the matter?"

"Nothing," Chuannan said. "I was just wondering about Eva."

"Well, I don't know if she's in on this, but I have no intention of seeing her until we're finished with this," Hu Dzem said. "After that, we'll take her to one of the other brothels and deal with her. First things first, though. Now, go."

Chuannan eyed the chairman and his bodyguard, then turned and headed back toward the elevators. His legs felt like lead. He thought back to his conversation with Jiang Yang the previous night. Hu Dzem had to be killed this morning, the sooner the better. Chuannan had had it all figured out, but now everything had changed. How could he even think about pulling off an assassination with everything else going on? It would be suicide. By the same token, he knew if he ignored Yang's orders and let Hu Dzem live, there would be consequences as well. He'd be a marked man in Yang's book. Either way he was screwed.

Chuannan pressed for the elevator. The doors opened. He stepped inside, feeling as if, one way or another, he was on the verge of sealing his doom.

What do I do? he wondered.

26

In his room at the White Orchid Inn, Sam Chen had the laptop set up next to the transceiver and had linked the two units by means of a USB connector, allowing the computer's software to read Molvico's radioed position and indicate his whereabouts within the diagrammed blueprint of the Dynasty. The blinking dot had remained in the reception area for some time, corresponding to Molvico's minicam view of the large room. Chen could see the bodyguard who had remained behind, and when Dee Wong returned from a second trip to the back room, he could see steam rising from the cup of tea she was bringing Molvico.

There was something about the way Wong was stirring the tea that raised a red flag for Chen. He knew it might be an idiosyncrasy on the woman's part, but to the best of Chen's recollection, at least nine times out of ten when he'd seen people serve tea they tugged on the string connected to the tea bag rather than bothering with a spoon. He'd heard Molvico ask for some liquor, but Chen suspected the drink had been spiked with another substance.

"Watch out for that tea," he warned Molvico, "I may be wrong, but I'm thinking they slipped in something besides booze, if you get my meaning."

Molvico wasn't in a position to respond directly, but Chen could see the other agent take the cup and raise it close enough to his face that the minicam image was briefly obscured by steam.

"Thanks, but I'm really sorry," Molvico told Dee Wong, "I should have told you. Green tea gives me hives."

Chen saw Wong's brow furrow briefly as she exchanged a look with the bodyguard before smiling her way back to Molvico's side to retrieve the tea, asking, "Another flavor perhaps?"

"Nah, that's okay." Molvico chuckled. "On second thought, I don't want this beer gut of mine to bloat out any more than it already is."

Wong continued to smile as she took the tea. Once she'd turned and headed toward the back room, Chen leaned toward the transceiver microphone and told Molvico, "Nice save, Terry. I don't know if drugging johns is normal with these people or if they're suspicious of you. Stay on your toes."

When Chen heard the door opening behind him, he didn't bother turning, assuming it was Wood.

"You might wanna hold off going for the car," he called out. "There's a chance we may have to abort and—"

Chen groaned as he felt a sudden stabbing pain in his back, accompanied by a shoving sensation that nearly knocked him from his chair. He threw his arms out at his sides, trying to keep his balance as he glanced over his shoulder, just in time to see Xiao Deng drawing bead on him with his Walther P-22. A makeshift silencer had muffled the first shot, and Chen barely heard the follow-up, a round to the face that snapped his head back and sent him reeling backward.

Xiao Deng lowered his gun and stepped around Chen's body, eyeing the transceiver. On the monitor, Molvico was still reacting to the disconcerting noises he'd just heard through his earplug, and the minicam image he was transmitting blurred as he looked around wildly. Once the image stabilized, Xiao was able to make out the interior of the Dynasty reception area.

"Clever," Deng muttered, grabbing his cell phone and thumbing a number with his free hand. "But not clever enough."

CHRISTINE WOOD WAS putting away her makeup and chiding herself for her vanity when she heard scuffling in the room next door, followed by the sound of something crashing to the floor.

She knew at once something was wrong. She yanked a Ruger Mark II .22LR suppressed pistol from its web holster as she headed for the door. She was reaching for the knob when she heard a card key being slipped into the outside lock. Wood instinctively went for the safety chain. She'd barely slipped the chain into place when the door swung inward, only to be brought to a sudden stop.

She recoiled from the door, catching a glimpse of the man on the other side. She didn't recognize him. When she spotted his gun, she raised her Ruger and fired. The .22-caliber round drilled into the doorjamb with enough force and noise to drive the man back momentarily.

Hung Deng, who'd lost precious seconds letting himself into the wrong suite adjacent to that shared by Chen and Molvico, cursed, then lunged against the door, shoulder first. The chain's brackets loosened, but the door still held.

Wood suspected her assailant's next attempt would involve a well-placed kick, gaining him entry. If she'd known for sure the man was alone, she might've held her ground and mowed him down once the door swung open, but she was concerned about being outnumbered.

I'm outta here, she told herself, bolting away from the door. There was a small television set on top of the dresser. Wood grabbed it with both hands and jerked it free of its plastic security mount, snapping the cord from the outlet. In nearly the same movement, she pivoted and let the set fly from her hands. A second later, the picture window overlooking

Hennessey Avenue shattered. Wood turned back and fired another round at the door, then rushed to the opening, raking the barrel of her Ruger across the window's inner framework to dislodge the remaining shards of glass.

The bounty hunter had one leg out the window when the door to her room imploded. She balanced herself on the sill, feeling a stray piece of glass bite into the underside of her leg. She ignored the pain and drew a quick bead on the intruder, putting two slugs into the assassin's chest before he could fire at her. He wasn't wearing any body armor and the shots brought him to his knees, his liver perforated by one bullet and his aortic valve creased by the other. He managed to get off a return shot but missed Wood by a good three yards.

A narrow ledge ran the entire length of the building's exterior and once Wood had both feet on the ledge, she clawed at the brick facade for support and began to inch her way toward Chen's room. Once she was close to the window, she reached out and swung hard so that the Ruger's butt hit the glass squarely, obliterating it.

Wood was about to show herself when a shot fired out the window, shattering still more glass. Having waited out the shot, Wood leaned to one side, at the same time shifting her pistol back into firing position. Peering in through the broken window, she was stunned at first to find herself staring at the man she thought she'd just killed in the other room.

It didn't seem possible, but there was no time to question logic. The man had backtracked to the main door and opened it, letting light from the hallway turn him into a living silhouette similar to the targets at the Inter-Trieve shooting range. She directed her fire at the hit man's neck and head. She was off balance so it took her three shots, but she'd taken out the gangster's carotid artery and splintered his lower jaw. He staggered backward and crumpled to the hall floor.

Wood was fairly sure the man was dead but wanted confirmation. She was pulling herself through the window when her attention drawn to Sam Chen, who lay still on the floor next to the toppled laptop, clearly beyond any hope of resuscitation.

"Bastards!" Wood swore.

There was no time for the woman to let her rage build. A bullet fired from street level kissed off the brickwork a few yards from her, stinging her face with chips of shrapnel. Whirling, she scanned the bustling street and spotted the shooter, a man dressed in bedraggled clothes standing next to a kiosk just outside the main entrance to the White Orchid.

There were more than a dozen pedestrians crowded around the kiosk and the coffee stand located next to it. Panic overcame them and they scattered in all directions, making it impossible for Wood to safely return fire. Instead, she glanced directly below her, then climbed out the window and pushed off, jumping feetfirst from the building.

A hotel awning helped break her fall, as did the handful of pedestrians she landed on.

"Sorry about that," she said, ignoring the startled cries as she bounded to her feet and scrambled past the remains of the television set she'd tossed out the window earlier.

The ragged gunman had moved from the kiosk and was shoving his way through the crowd toward Wood. She took cover behind a postal bin and waved frantically at the pedestrians around her. "Get the hell out of the way!" she shouted.

When the shooter saw that Wood wasn't about to go down easily, he reached out and grabbed an elderly Chinese man dressed in a baggy gray suit. Using the man for a human shield, the shooter pointed his pistol at the old man's head, then dragged him from the sidewalk into the street. Traffic had come to a stop and the gunman threaded his way between cars, ignoring the bray of horns and curses being hurled at him by several drivers. One man shifted his Jetta into park and was getting out of the car when the gunman turned on him and pulled the trigger, dropping him to the street.

Wood had moved out into the street in time to see the killing, but there was still no way for her to get off a safe shot. To her surprise, however, she saw the man go down before he could plant his gun back against the temple of the old man he was holding captive. On a hunch, Wood looked across the street. A member of the Inter-Trieve backup team had climbed up onto the roof of the panel truck parked in front of the Dynasty, providing himself a clear shot at the assassin.

"Good job, Mitch!" Wood called out, raising her voice above the din.

The other agent nodded to her and was about to climb down from the truck when he suddenly pitched forward, gunned down by a sniper posted on the roof of a souvenir shop located directly next door to the White Orchid. Wood spotted the man and crouched behind the nearest car idling in the traffic jam. When she saw the rifleman taking aim at her, she squeezed off a few shots. At least one of them found flesh. The sniper's rifle clattered to the sidewalk as the shot sent him plummeting to the concrete.

Sirens were wailing in the distance. Wood could see the lights of approaching squad cars. She zigzagged through the stalled traffic until she'd reached the other side of the street. Another Inter-Trieve agent had clambered out of the panel truck to check on Mitch Carlisle, who was stirring in the gutter where he'd fallen.

"I'm going to sneak in and check on things," she told the other agent. "If you can get Mitch in the truck, start the engine and be ready in case Terry and I come rushing out with Eva."

"Got it," the other agent responded.

Wood rushed along the sidewalk and ducked into the alley. There, a late model Porsche had just come to a stop and a man with a crew cut was getting out, gun in hand. Wood took aim at him and shouted, "Freeze!"

Ling Thieu responded by darting into a side doorway, then

peering back around the edge long enough to fire at Wood. She threw herself to the ground. The shots whizzed past her, one of them shattering the side window of one of the cars caught up in the traffic snarl. Wood was getting ready to fire back when she heard the door slam shut. The triggerman had obviously fled inside the brothel. She doubted he'd left the door unlocked, so, rising to her feet, she cast her eyes on the fire escape she'd photographed the previous night. The bottommost ladder was retracted, clamped in place beneath the second-story landing.

Sizing up the side of the building, the bounty hunter saw a way up and went for it. She holstered her pistol and stepped onto the sill of a ground-floor window, then clawed with one hand at the mortar work between the bricks that made up the building's edifice. With the other hand she reached up for the grillework of the fire escape landing.

"Damn it!" she cursed, realizing that she was a good foot and a half from being able to secure a grip and pull herself up. Her only option was to coil her legs as best she could and leap upward. If she missed, she'd have to try again or search out another way in. With lives at stake inside the building, she knew she couldn't afford to waste time. Wood crouched on the windowsill and was about to jump when she heard a second car enter the alley and squeeze past the Porsche. The driver slammed on the brakes just shy of the fire escape and threw his door open. Glancing through the windshield, Wood saw that the driver, like the man in the Porsche, was armed.

"Just what I don't need," she fumed.

Dropping to the asphalt, Christine quickly pulled her gun and swung it back into firing position. Finger on the trigger, she was about to shoot when she caught herself.

"It's about time you showed up," she called out to the man hunched behind the Chevy's door frame.

"I DON'T FEEL SO WELL all of a sudden," Molvico said, rising from his chair in the reception area. His earphone had picked up Sam Chen's dying gasp as well as the sounds of struggle in the hotel room. He knew the mission was in trouble.

The bodyguard posted by the elevators yanked out his gun and told Molvico, "Sit down!"

Dee Wong set Molvico's tea on her desktop and reached into a drawer, coming up with a pistol of her own. Outnumbered, Molvico eased back into the chair, grimacing. He doubled over slightly, clutching his stomach with one hand.

"My ulcer," he complained, discreetly reaching behind his back for his SIG-Sauer P-226.

"Hands up!" the hostess commanded, aiming her weapon at Molvico's forehead. "Now!"

"What is this?" Molvico said, bluffing. "I have an ulcer, damn it! What's with the guns?"

Dee Wong fired a warning round between Molvico's legs, lodging the bullet in the chair's padded framework, then raised the gun and repeated, "Hands up!"

"Okay!" Molvico said, extending his arms out at his sides.

Just then the front door swung open and a middle-aged couple rushed in, breathless. "There's shooting in the street!" the woman cried.

"Holy shit!" her husband gasped, seeing guns in the hands of Wong and the bodyguard and realizing they'd blundered from the frying pan into the fire.

"Get out!" the bodyguard yelled, striding toward the couple.

The couple fell over each other scrambling back toward the doorway. At the same time the bodyguard was shoving them out into the street and bolting the front door, the elevators opened behind Dee Wong. When the hostess turned to see Li Chuannan emerge from the elevator, Molvico made his move.

Lunging from his chair, the operative reached behind him.

By the time he'd hit the floor and rolled to one side, he had his pistol in hand.

Wong clipped him in the leg with a round from her weapon. Molvico returned the favor, pumping her in the chest with a 9 mm slug. The woman let out a cry and fell sideways across her desk, spilling tea and sending a vase crashing to the floor.

The bodyguard turned on Molvico and fired, putting two slugs into the field op's upper chest and left shoulder. Molvico grimaced as he crawled past Wong and took cover behind the desk, leaving a trail of blood in his wake. He shot at the bodyguard, forcing the other man to dive to one side and seek refuge behind one of the stone columns framing the entryway foyer.

Li Chuannan, meanwhile, froze in front of the elevator, grappling with the realization that yet another monkey wrench had been thrown into his plans. It wasn't until Molvico turned to him and leveled his SIG-Sauer that the enforcer willed himself into motion, backpedaling into the elevator. A gunshot thundered in after him, taking out one of the mirrored walls. Chuannan frantically stabbed at the controls until the doors hissed closed, then pressed for the top floor. He figured the farther he got from the firefight, the more time he'd have to figure a way out of his nightmare. Somewhere in his mind, he knew that if Hu Dzem was still in his penthouse, he might still be able to kill the chairman and somehow live to tell the tale.

THE MOMENT HE ENTERED the building, Ling Thieu heard gunshots in the reception area. He assumed Li Chuannan was carrying out Jiang Yang's orders and wondered why the bouncer had made his move downstairs instead of confronting Hu Dzem in his office. He was reaching for the inner door leading to the first-floor hallway when he caught himself and stopped. The shooting hadn't stopped, and Thieu could tell there was more than one gun being fired. He figured Li Chuannan had run into resistance and he was wary of throwing himself into the fray. It was bad enough Yang had sent him as the bouncer's backup. Thieu wasn't about to risk his neck getting caught up in Chuannan's blundering. Better, he figured, to wait things out. Once the shooting stopped, he could show himself and see what kind of mess had been left for him to tend to.

Thieu was lingering outside the door when he heard glass breaking in the stairwell just above him.

"What now?" he muttered, taking to the stairs and heading up to the second floor. He stopped on the landing between floors. The woman he'd just fired at in the alleyway was climbing in through the broken window leading to the fire escape. Thieu raised his pistol, determined to finish her off.

WOOD HAD CLEARED the window and was making room for the Executioner when Thieu's .357 Magnum pistol thundered in the stairwell. A slug rocketed past Wood's ear, taking a chunk of concrete out of the wall behind her. She whirled to one side and backpedaled out of the line of fire.

Bolan heard the shot, and when he came in through the window, he was ready with his Beretta. He spotted Thieu on the midfloor landing and targeted him with a 3-round burst. Thieu wasted a shot on the staircase in front of him as he staggered backward, clipped in the chest. His legs gave out beneath him and he slumped to the floor, clutching at his wounds.

Bolan hurried down the steps, gun trained on the man with the crew cut. Wood was right behind him. They could both hear the ongoing firefight in the reception area.

"One of my guys is part of that," Wood told Bolan. "I'm gonna go see if I can—"

Wood's voice trailed off as she realized the steel door leading to the ground floor corridor was locked. She kicked it in frustration. Bolan, meanwhile, grabbed the Magnum pistol from Thieu and stared into the dying man's eyes.

"Is Yang here?" he demanded.

Thieu stared back at Bolan, eyes filled with hate. Summoning what little strength he had left in him, he spit at the Executioner. Bolan ignored the taunt and was about to repeat his question when he realized he wouldn't be getting any answers. The life had already gone out of Thieu's eyes.

"He's gone," Bolan said, rising.

"Well, we're not," Wood said. "Let's try the next floor and see if we can wrap this up."

IN THE RECEPTION AREA, Terrance Molvico was losing blood fast. His wounds filled him with a burning sensation whenever he moved, but he blocked the pain from his mind and gritted his teeth, resolved to fight on. He traded shots with the bodyguard but stuck to single rounds while the other man carved away at the desk with autobursts. The strategy paid off. When there was a sudden lull in their exchange, Molvico guessed that the bodyguard had run out of ammo. Grimacing, he rose to a crouch and risked breaking cover. He staggered across the carpet to a point where he had a clearer aim at the bodyguard, who was in the process of ramming a fresh cartridge into his pistol.

"Waste not, want not," Molvico said, plugging the other man with a pair of kill shots, one to the heart, the other to the head. The guard went down hard, taking one of the potted plants with him.

Weak from the battle, Molvico sagged against the desk to steady himself. A numbness began to come over him, so he lowered himself to his knees. He continued to lose strength as he struggled to slip his coat off so he could get a better look at the shots he'd taken in the chest. When he heard someone coming in through the rear entrance, he stopped what he was doing and raised his gun. Moments later, a uniformed police officer charged into view, both hands on his pistol as he swept the room.

Slaughter House

"It's over," Molvico said, hoping the cop could speak some English. "But I could use a medic."

The cop eyed Dee Wong and the fallen bodyguard, then turned to Molvico. Molvico didn't like the look in the other man's eyes, and when the cop pointed his gun at him, the Inter-Trieve operative began to have his doubts that the cavalry had come to the rescue. Before he could react and bring his gun into play, however, Shu Ter-Ci calmly pulled the trigger, hastening Molvico's slide to the grave.

"*Now* it's over," the cop said as he watched Molvico drop to the carpet next to Dee Wong.

27

The rooms in the Dynasty, like those in most upscale brothels, were thoroughly soundproofed, so Eva Kelmin had no idea the building was under siege and that the ground floor had been turned into a war zone. The double-ply glass windows, however, could not fully mute the sounds of the street, and the blaring horns and intermittent gunfire had drawn the teenaged runaway's attention to the skirmish playing out on Hennessey Avenue.

Staring out at the bedlam, Eva sensed the battle was somehow linked to the Dynasty. She had yet to be given any signal to proceed with her plan to kill Hu Dzem, so her first assumption was that a power struggle between the chairman and some rival faction had just come to a head. She also assumed that her freedom had suddenly become a matter of secondary importance to Li Chuannan. Like it or not, Eva figured she was once again on her own.

Mesmerized as she was by the tumult in the street, Eva tore herself from the window and began to pace frantically. Part of her ached for the call from Chuannan, but she felt relieved that she might not be called upon to carry out the execution of Hu Dzem. She despised the man and would have liked nothing more than to see him dead, but she had never held a gun in her life, much less turned it on someone and pulled the trigger. Even with her freedom at stake, she wasn't sure she'd be up to the task.

Eva was still grappling with her dilemma when someone

began to pound on her door. She flinched and let out an involuntary gasp, figuring it had to be Chuannan.

She was wrong.

"Eva! Open up! It's me!" a woman called out from the other side of the door. Eva recognized the voice as that of Taddie Lancaster, a twenty-year-old New Zealander who'd been working—also against her will—at the Dynasty for three months. Taddie had bonded with Eva during the week she'd been at the brothel, and the two of them had shared a number of secret conversations bemoaning their fate and wondering when and how they might be able to one day put it behind them. Eva rushed to the door and opened it. Taddie was tall, blond and blue-eyed, and wore nothing but a pastel blue silk slip.

"All hell's broken loose!" she whispered urgently. "I don't know what's going on, but maybe there's a chance we can run for it. What do you say?"

"I...I don't know," Eva stammered.

"It's worth a try!" Taddie urged, grabbing Eva by the hand. "Come on!"

"My things—"

"There's no time for that!" Taddie insisted. "Come on!"

Eva reluctantly followed Taddie into the hallway, still bewildered by the ever-changing events she'd been caught up in. Her room was next to the elevators, and she instinctively pushed the button.

"No!" Taddie cried out, tugging Eva the other way. "We'll take the stairs. It'll probably be safer."

The young woman hurried down the hall. They were about enter the stairwell when the door suddenly swung open on them. They both let out a cry as a man and woman charged into the hallway, nearly colliding with them.

"Eva!" Christine Wood exclaimed. "What do you know, something's finally gone right around here!"

Eva stared at Wood and Mack Bolan, unnerved by the sight of the guns they were wielding.

"Who are—"

"Your father sent us to bring you home," Wood interrupted. "That's all you need to know right now. Let's go!"

Bolan held the door to the stairwell open for the women.

The former captives were heading past Wood and Bolan into the stairwell when the elevator doors opened at the far end of the hall. Li Chuannan appeared, gun in hand, clearly annoyed that the elevator had stopped a floor shy of the penthouse. When he saw Eva and Taddie being led away by their would-be rescuers, his expression suddenly changed to one of unchecked rage.

"No, you don't!" he shouted, raising his Tokarev and squeezing off a burst.

The Executioner was a step ahead of the bouncer. He'd already shoved Taddie and Eva into the stairwell. Letting the door close behind him, he lurched to one side, sidestepping Chuannan's pistol rounds. Wood did the same, pressing herself against the opposite wall.

Bolan swung his Beretta into play, returning fire. Chuannan remained in the elevator, using the thick metal frame for cover. As he had on the ground floor, he pressed the *close* button, then got off another quick volley before the doors hissed shut, absorbing rounds meant for him.

Bolan glanced at the light panel above the elevators and saw that Chuannan was going up.

"Take the girls," he told Wood as he yanked the stairwell door open. "I'm going after—"

Bolan suddenly fell silent as he saw Wood fold to her knees, one hand grasping at her chest. Blood was already beginning to seep through her fingers.

"Bastard nicked me," she groaned.

All thought of pursuing Li Chuannan fell by the wayside as Bolan dropped to one knee and caught Wood as she lost consciousness and pitched forward. When her hand fell clear of her chest, Bolan saw that her blouse was soaked with blood. Easing her onto the carpet, he ripped at her blouse while shouting over his shoulder, "I need some help!"

Eva and Taddie rushed back into the corridor and stared with horror as Bolan dropped his Beretta and pressed both hands against Wood's wound, trying to stop the bleeding.

"Hang in there," he whispered.

"Oh, my God," Eva gasped. "Is she dead?"

Bolan ignored the question. "Do either of you know how to use a gun?" he asked.

"I do," Taddie said.

Bolan nodded toward his fallen pistol. "Take mine and keep us covered," he said.

He turned to Eva and quickly added, "I need you down here."

Eva dropped to her knees, queasy at the sight of so much blood.

"Take over for me," he told her. "You need to keep pressure on the wound, all right?"

Eva nodded and placed her hands next to Bolan's.

"Now," he told her, removing his hands.

Eva began to weep as she cupped one palm securely over the wound and used her other hand to increase the pressure.

"What's happening here?" Taddie asked, her voice trembling as she kept an eye on the hallway.

"Quiet!" Bolan said. He'd clasped one hand around Wood's wrist and was checking for a pulse. He couldn't find one. She was losing color, her skin going pale. He leaned close to her face, brushing his cheek close to her lips, hoping to feel her breathing. Nothing.

"Keep steady pressure on that wound," he told Eva. "I need to try CPR."

As he continued his attempts to get Wood's heart to start beating, however, the Executioner could feel a cold emptiness well up inside him. He finished the compressions and checked again to see if Wood was breathing.

Still nothing.

He went back to rescue breathing. Two fruitless breaths later, Bolan's hope began to fade. He was running out of time.

LI CHUANNAN SNAPPED.

The stress of moment—coupled with the quick trigger his daily steroid dose had placed on his temper—left the Dynasty enforcer in a blind rage as he stormed from the elevator and stalked down the top-floor hallway. The grand finesse of his master plan to eliminate Hu Dzem was a distant memory, lost in the chaos that had turned the brothel into a shooting gallery. Equally lost were any notions of self-preservation Chuannan had harbored when he'd fled the shootout on the ground floor. He was consumed by one thought and one thought only: to kill Hu Dzem and anyone who got in the way of his carrying out the execution.

There was no one in the hallway and the door to the chairman's office was closed. Chuannan figured Hu Dzem had turned the dead bolt to lock himself in after witnessing the downstairs mayhem on his surveillance cameras, so he didn't bother trying the door. Instead, he holstered his gun and turned his attention to a three-foot-high bronze replica of Rodin's *The Kiss* resting on a walnut pedestal between two potted dracaenas.

The statue weighed more than a hundred pounds, but with adrenaline stoking his furor, Chuannan wrested the art piece from the stand as if it were made of balsa. Torquing his body, he gathered some momentum, then sent the statue crashing into the tinted floor-to-ceiling glass wall next to the office doorway. Though reinforced and bulletproof, the wall was no match for the hurtled projectile and the glass shattered in a shower of gleaming beads the size of breath mints.

Chest heaving, sweat pouring down his reddened face, Chuannan drew his Tokarev and charged through the opening. As he'd hoped, the disintegration of the wall had taken both Hu Dzem and his bodyguard by surprise. Chuannan went for the guard first, getting off two quick shots before the antiquated pistol jammed on him. The guard dropped his gun without firing it and collapsed to the floor, both slugs imbedded in what remained of his skull.

Hu Dzem, who'd been in the process of emptying the contents of a wall safe into a tooled-leather valise, glared wildly at Chuannan. "What's the meaning of this?" he shouted.

Chuannan said nothing. He struggled to unjam his gun, and when it refused to cooperate he roared with frustration and hurled the weapon at Hu Dzem. The chairman reflexively threw up his left arm and the weapon glanced off his wrist.

Hu Dzem let out a roar and reached into the safe for a 9 mm Luger, determined to gun down his enforcer while he was unarmed. When he turned back to Chuannan, however, he saw that the other man was now brandishing a small derringer.

"Jiang Yang sends his regards," Chuannan said as he fired the weapon he'd hidden in the office for Eva Kelmin to use on the chairman.

"You traitor—"

Hu Dzem was silenced when the minigun's jacketed round bored through his neck, taking out his voice box, Adam's apple and a portion of his upper spine.

Chuannan stared numbly as he watched the chairman slump over his desk. Like a wisp of smoke, the bouncer's rage immediately began to fade, giving way to an eerie sense of calm.

He'd done it. He'd killed Hu Dzem.

His mission accomplished, Chuannan's mind cleared. With an ease that surprised him, he realized what his next move should be. First he snatched up both Hu Dzem's Luger and the Walther dropped by the chairman's bodyguard. He then started to empty the rest of Hu Dzem's valuables from the safe into the valise. He was so distracted by the hoard of wealth that he didn't hear Shu Ter-Ci enter until the rogue cop's crepe soles crunched down on the glass that had once been the office wall. Ter-Ci stared at Hu Dzem's corpse with disbelief, then glanced up at Chuannan.

"What happened here?" he demanded.

"What does it look like?"

Chuannan drowned out his own words with a burst from the Luger. Shu Ter-Ci raised his gun but was dead before he could fire. He toppled forward, landing on the statue Chuannan had heaved through the glass.

Chuannan quickly shoveled the rest of the safe's contents into the valise, then tossed in the Luger before slamming it shut and tucking it under his arm. Reaching beneath Hu Dzem's desk, he groped the underside of the desktop until his fingers brushed against two toggle switches. One worked a silent alarm.

Chuannan flicked the second switch.

Behind him, a dull sound came from within the paneled wall. When Chuannan tugged at the sconce lamp mounted to the paneling, a portion of the wall moved on unseen hinges, revealing a closet-sized cavity.

Wary of police raids, Hu Dzem had had a private elevator installed in his office several years earlier, and it was during one such raid that Chuannan had learned how to access the secret shaft.

Once inside the dimly lit enclosure, Li Chuannan pressed a button, then began his descent to a chamber located beneath the ground floor of the Dynasty. Once he reached the chamber, the bouncer knew he would be able to take a narrow passageway that ran beneath Hennessey Avenue all the way to a heavily wooded section of Southorn Park. From there, he'd have to play it by ear. But at least he would be free.

28

Although the triads had deeply infiltrated the Hong Kong police department, the force was still, on the whole, beyond their influence, and all seven of the squad cars that converged on the Dynasty in the wake of the bloodbath were manned by officers loyal to their oaths. Half of them fell to the task of restoring order on Hennessey Avenue. The others stormed the brothel, guns at the ready.

After surveying the carnage in the reception area, they spread out and began to search the rest of the premises floor-by-floor. Three officers wound up on the second story, where they found four scantily clad women huddled anxiously around Mack Bolan, who was still crouched over Christine Wood, attempting yet another round of CPR. One of the cops was fluent in English. Seeing the look of exhaustion on Bolan's face, he motioned the prostitutes aside and knelt beside him.

"How long have you been trying to resuscitate her?" the cop asked.

Bolan finished his series of compressions, then stared at Wood's lifeless features. The woman's skin had taken on a bluish tinge. "Too long," he said, his voice hoarse.

The cop barked for another officer to call for paramedics, then began to roll up his sleeves. "I'll take over," he said.

Bolan let out a weary breath and shook his head, resigned to the inevitable.

"It's too late," he said. "She's gone."

Bolan slowly rose from his knees, eyes still on the woman he'd been unable to save. He could feel a tightness in his chest nearly as pronounced as the sudden emptiness in his soul.

"Your partner?" the cop asked him.

Bolan shook his head again. "A colleague," he said.

Taddie and Eva were hugging each other, weeping. The other two women were less demonstrative but clearly in a state of shock.

"I'm sorry," Eva sputtered, mascara running down her cheeks as she stared at Bolan. "She came here to rescue me and—"

The runaway couldn't finish. She looked at Wood and fresh tears welled in her eyes.

"You're safe now," Bolan told her. Gesturing at Wood, he added, "She'll take that with her."

Bolan showed the cops his ID, then picked up his Beretta off the floor where Taddie had set it a few minutes before.

"We have the building locked down," the officer told Bolan. "Leave matters to us."

Bolan stared hard at the officer.

"I want the man who did this," he said matter-of-factly. "Don't try to stop me."

The officer stared back at Bolan but said nothing. Finally he turned and spoke to another one of the cops, then told Bolan, "Let him go with you."

Bolan knew it was a smart move. With other officers roaming about, he might stumble into a situation where they would feel the need to shoot first and ask questions later.

"Thank you," he told the officer. He explained who Eva Kelmin was and secured assurances that a close watch would be kept on her until arrangements could be made to have her flown to San Francisco.

Over the course of the next half hour, Bolan took part in the floor-by-floor search for Li Chuannan. The bouncer didn't turn up, and by the time one of the officers chanced upon the desk switch operating the trick panel leading to Hu Dzem's secret elevator, the Executioner knew that Wood's killer was long gone. The realization tore at him.

Told that Wood's body was about to be driven to the morgue, Bolan excused himself and made his way out of the building. Traffic was still heavy on Hennessey Avenue, and the sidewalks were congested with curiosity-seekers as well as the hundreds of witnesses who'd been detained for routine questioning. In addition to the patrol cars, there were four paramedic vans double-parked in front the Dynasty. Other vehicles had already left to take the wounded to the hospital. Those remaining would be transporting the dead.

Bits of information were being pieced together by the officers, and Bolan learned that in addition to Christine Wood, four other Inter-Trieve agents had been killed in the firefight, including Terrance Molvico, Mitch Carlisle and Sam Chen. As in Jotuwi, it was a heavy toll, one that overshadowed the fact that Eva Kelmin had been rescued.

29

Stony Man Farm, Virginia

"How's it coming, gang?" Aaron Kurtzman asked, wheeling his way into the Computer Room, refreshed after an hour-long catnap. When he'd left, Akira Tokaido had just learned of a report that a parachutist had splash-landed near a private beach resort on Hainan Island. The Stony Man cyberteam had leaped on the news, figuring the odds were that the chutist was Jiang Yang. They'd also decided to work on the assumption that the Hong Kong gangster had chosen the resort as his drop point more by design than accident. Over the past hour, Tokaido, Carmen Delahunt and Hunt Wethers had teamed up to methodically search every available database looking for some connection between Yang and the resort. Their work had not been in vain.

"We hit the jackpot," Delahunt reported.

"Yeah?" Kurtzman said as he stopped to fire up a fresh pot of coffee. "Let's hear it."

"First off," Delahunt began, "the resort is owned by a billionaire named Ki Dan. He got in on the ground floor when China opened up Hainan to gaming and pretty much cornered the market. This is just one of four casinos he runs along the south coast of the island. The guy's richer than God."

Kurtzman nodded, taking in the information. "His name

rings a bell. He's got his fingers in some other pies besides gambling, doesn't he?"

"He's invested all over the place," Tokaido interjected, referring to the information on his computer screen. "Everything from properties to publishing. But when it comes to linking him with Yang, there's his manufacturing holdings. The plant that made that centrifuge Yang's people were trying to peddle down in Jotuwi Port is Ki Dan's."

"Of course, we had to sift through a handful of shell companies before we made the connection," Wethers added. "He's a least five times removed from any association."

"Stands to reason," Kurtzman said. "Gotta figure a guy like that's going to be savvy about covering his tracks."

"He almost pulled it off," Tokaido said. "We were down to our last search engine when he finally popped up on the radar."

"I'll remember that next time Hal complains about us wanting more funds to beef up our databases," Kurtzman noted.

"Good idea," Tokaido said.

"Okay, then," Kurtzman went on. "We've got Yang dropping in on Ki Dan. Is he still at the resort?"

"No confirmation on that yet," Tokaido said. "UNMO sent a team there to ask questions, but everyone at the resort's being tight-lipped. All we know for sure is that security fished Yang out of the surf after he landed and then whisked him away from some party for high rollers on the beach."

"You're forgetting," Delahunt reminded Tokaido, "we also have Ki Dan down as being in the Philippines on business, which means Yang's on hold in terms of seeing the guy."

"Right," Tokaido conceded. He went on. "Anyway, if Yang's not cooling his heels at the resort, they might've moved him to one of Dan's other properties. If that's the case, we're in for some work, because besides the other casinos, Dan has an estate up the coast along with an apartment and private yacht down in Sanya. Throw in the manufacturing plants and his other businesses and there's a ton of ground to cover."

"We're trying to coordinate manpower to check out every option," Delahunt pitched in, "but it's tricky because we need to do an end run around the Chinese authorities."

"Ki Dan has them in his pocket, no doubt," Kurtzman surmised.

"Exactly," the redhead replied.

"Another option we need to consider is that Yang's already left the island for Hong Kong," Kurtzman said. "After all, he's got some answering to do with Hu Dzem and the triad, right?"

"Actually," Wethers said, "we're ruling that out. Our feeling is that by going to Ki Dan, Yang is cutting ties with San Hop Kwan."

Kurtzman frowned as he sipped his coffee. "Why's that?" he asked.

"Two reasons," Wethers responded. "For starters, after everything that went down in Malaysia, you have to figure Yang's stock with the triad is in the toilet. He left such a mess back there it's not likely he'll be able to salvage any kind of standing with the organization."

"Perhaps," Kurtzman conceded. "On the other hand, we've run across other guys like this who've weathered worse storms and found a way to come out smelling like a rose."

"True enough," Wethers said, "but in this case we don't think that will happen. It has to do with some bad blood between Ki Dan and Hu Dzem that we managed to dig up."

Wethers deferred to Delahunt, who'd come across the information and had it called up on her computer screen.

"It's linked to the gambling licenses in Hainan," Delahunt said. "When the island was initially green-lighted for casinos, Hu Dzem figured he was first in line, given the way he was wired into the gambling rackets in Hong Kong and on the mainland. When he found out Ki Dan had thrown around some money and cut in ahead of him, Hu Dzem didn't take it very well. As a matter of fact, he put a contract out on Ki Dan, and from what we've dredged up, there were at least two attempts to take the guy out. Obviously, both failed, but Ki Dan lost four bodyguards in the process, not to mention a niece who's still comatose after catching a bullet in her spine when some of Dzem's thugs opened up on her wedding ceremony."

Kurtzman absorbed this latest wrinkle as he finished his first cup of coffee and started in on a second.

"I see your point," he told Wethers. "It seems a pretty safe bet that if Yang's gone to see Ki Dan, it's to jump ship."

"That and to provide information that would help Ki Dan get back at Hu Dzem," Tokaido added. "Mr. Moneybags is on record as saying he wants Hu Dzem dead."

"No surprise there," Kurtzman said.

"He just got his wish," Barbara Price said. The mission controller had just entered the Computer Room, a solemn look on her face. "Hu Dzem was just murdered at his headquarters in Hong Kong."

"That was fast," Tokaido said.

"Wait a second," Kurtzman said. "Wasn't Hu Dzem working out of the same brothel where that Kelmin girl was supposedly being held?"

Price nodded. "She's free now," she said, her voice flat. "Striker was there lending a hand. Christine Wood is dead," Price reported. "There was a shootout. Her entire team went down."

Silence fell over the Computer Room as the cyber team reacted to the news.

Kurtzman wanted to ask how Bolan was and how he'd taken the news, but he refrained. He could well imagine, however, what the Executioner's frame of mind had to be like in light of what had happened.

"Whoever this triggerman is," he said, "I can guarantee you that his days on this planet are numbered."

Hong Kong

ONCE HE'D EMERGED from the getaway passage into the woods of Southorn Park, Li Chuannan flagged down a taxi for the short ride to Victoria Harbour. On the way, he'd fought back an urge to open the valise and get an estimate of the plunder he'd absconded with from Hu Dzem's safe. There would be time for that later, he figured. Besides, he felt the need to keep his eyes on the surrounding traffic, wary the police might somehow catch up with him before he could fully distance himself from the scene of the crime. Several squad cars had driven past the taxi, roof lights flashing, but they hadn't pulled the cab over and Chuannan figured they were bound for the Dynasty.

The bouncer got out of the taxi at the ferry port. As he stood in line before the ticket booth, he weighed his options. Even without counting, he knew there was enough cash in the valise to allow him to forget about the triad and any plans to hook up with Jiang Yang. He was rich enough to live like a king for the rest of his life. The catch, however, was that once San Hop Kwan had pegged him as Hu Dzem's killer, Chuannan knew they would come looking for him. He could probably go underground, move far from Hong Kong and buy himself a new identity, but if the triad was determined to find him, there would be no smoke screen thick enough to hide behind. Going it alone wasn't the answer.

Finally Chuannan reached the front of the line.

"Where to?" the ticket person asked.

Chuannan knew there was only one course open to him, one place he could go where he might be safe from retaliation by the San Hop Kwan.

"Hainan," he told the ticket person.

Hainan Island, China

THE NEWS OF HU DZEM'S death reached Ki Dan's estate in three stages.

Less than two minutes after Jiang Yang had received a call from Li Chuannan on his cell phone, Dan's sources in Hong Kong had confirmed the bouncer's story, and five minutes after that, both Yang and Dan were watching news coverage of the Dynasty shootout on a huge plasma screen in the billionaire's lavishly appointed den. Both men had changed, Dan into a white linen business suit, Yang into a borrowed pair of tan slacks and dress shirt. Dan's face bore a look of quiet satisfaction as he stared at the videotaped footage of Hu Dzem's body being taken from the brothel on a stretcher by local paramedics.

"Justice is served," he whispered.

Yang was still in the dark as to why Ki Dan had wanted Hu Dzem killed, but he was no longer hungry to have his curiosity fed with the details. All that mattered to him was that he'd fulfilled his end of the bargain with Dan. He'd earned a place on the billionaire's payroll and was ready to determine just what kind of deal he could cut for himself to insure that'd made the right choice in defecting from the triad.

"So," he prompted Ki Dan, "now that we've settled this matter, let's get down to business."

"What's your hurry?" Dan asked him.

A valet entered the den, carrying a tray with a bottle of champagne and two fluted glasses. Ki Dan motioned for the valet to set the tray on the table in front of him, then waved the man away. Once they were alone, he took the bottle and began to fill the two glasses.

"We can get down to business soon enough," the billionaire told Yang. "For now, let's celebrate. Today is a good day."

30

Hong Kong

"Man's in a serious funk," Jack Grimaldi said, staring out through the glass door leading to the balcony of the hotel suite he and Kissinger had encamped at after arriving in Hong Kong. John Kissinger stood nearby, packing the last of his things. He glanced over his shoulder and saw Mack Bolan out on the balcony, staring out at city. The Executioner hadn't changed position for nearly twenty minutes.

"Can't blame him," Kissinger observed. "Hell, he says they barely exchanged more than a few words before going into the building, then the next thing he knows, she's gone and he can't bring her back. That's a heavy load."

Grimaldi nodded. "Yeah, and it's not like this is the first time he's had to go through this. He'll need some time."

"Maybe so," Kissinger said, "but you know as well as me that he's not going to take it. Not as long as the guy who offed her is still out there somewhere."

On that front, although Wood's killer had been identified as Dynasty bouncer Li Chuannan, the ex-wrestler's trail had gone cold once his footprints had led authorities to a jogging path running through Southorn Park. The park was being canvassed for possible witnesses who might have seen the man after he emerged from the getaway tunnel, and dispatchers from all local taxi companies had been asked to check with their drivers to see if Chuannan had been one of their fares. All trains, boats and planes leaving Hong Kong had been alerted to be on the lookout for the killer as well, but both Grimaldi and Kissinger knew all these tasks would be time-consuming, with a good chance of proving as fruitless as their earlier visit to Jiang Yang's strip mall office.

"There's one stone we didn't overturn," Grimaldi said, thinking back on the office raid. He fished through his pockets and pulled out the business card of one of the Hong Kong police officers they'd turned the secretary over to, along with the evidence linking Yang to the aborted centrifuge transaction in Malaysia. As he dialed the number on the card, he told Kissinger, "I'm gonna have 'em ask that secretary if Yang had any ties to Chuannan."

"Couldn't hurt," Kissinger said.

As Grimaldi's call was being transferred to the officer in question, Kissinger's attention was drawn to Bolan's notebook computer, which was propped open on the dining-room table. A dispatch had arrived from Akira Tokaido.

"Hot damn," he said, reading the update.

Grimaldi, meanwhile, wrapped up his call and clicked off his cell. He had a grin on his face. "They've been grilling her since they brought her in and she's already put Chuannan and Jiang Yang together," he reported. "It gets better, too. They just got a positive ID on Chuannan from a ticket seller for one of the ferry lines at Victoria Harbour. Seems our man bought himself a one-way ticket to Hainan Island. The only down side is that the ferry's already docked in Sanya and the passengers have all disembarked."

"I don't think they'll find him in Sanya," Kissinger said, glancing up from the computer. "My money says he left there the moment he got off the boat and started up the coast."

"What makes you say that?" Grimaldi said.

"Just got word from the Farm," Kissinger said. "It looks

like Jiang Yang has switched loyalties from the triad to some billionaire by the name of Ki Dan. Apparently the guy owns Hainan Island the way Capone used to own Chicago. At first they thought he was in the Philippines on business, but they just got word he changed plans at the last minute and flew back in a private chopper in the middle of the night."

"To meet with Yang?"

"That'd be my guess," Kissinger said.

"Where's the rendezvous?"

"Ki Dan has his own heliport at his estate on the island," Kissinger stated. "It's about an hour's drive from the casino Yang parachuted down to after he ditched us midair. You gotta think Yang's already there, with Li Chuannan on the way to join the party."

"Hot damn is right!" Grimaldi said excitedly.

The sound was loud enough to carry all the way out to the balcony and shake Bolan from his grim mulling. The Executioner slowly rose from his chair and what inside. One look at Grimaldi and Kissinger and he knew something was up.

"We're outta here," Grimaldi told Bolan, shutting off the notebook and lowering its lid. "We've got some logistics to work out, but it looks like you're going to have yourself a chance to kill two birds with one stone."

31

Stony Man Farm, Virginia

"Done," Aaron Kurtzman said, hanging up the phone at his station in the Stony Man Computer Room. "The Satcam will be on-target by the time they reach the island."

"It pays to have some clout, eh?" Brognola said, rubbing a kink in his neck. The big Fed had just returned from the White House, where he'd heard first hand—along with the President—that Eva Kelmin had been freed from her captors and would soon be home with her father.

It wasn't until he'd been briefed in the Computer Room, however, that he'd learned that the runaway's freedom had come at a cost every bit as high as the toll exacted during the firefight in Malaysia, if not more. Having absorbed the news, he, along with all the other gathered members of the Stony Man inner circle, were now focused on one priority: seeing to it that Mack Bolan would have first crack at bringing Li Chuannan and Jiang Yang to justice.

The official position was that Bolan's mission was to apprehend the triad gangsters so that they could be brought to trial for the spate of crimes linked to them over the past forty-eight hours. But Brognola knew that Bolan would not be content to leave the fate of his adversaries in the hands of the judicial system.

Kurtzman put the first phase of the plan into motion. Just as it had provided long-range aerial surveillance of the Jotuwi Port salvage yard, the NSA Orion spy satellite, which normally monitored the Indian Ocean, would transmit a steady stream of Satcam photos of Ki Dan's rambling coastal estate on Hainan Island. Other forces were being brought into play as well.

"Any word from UNMO?" Brognola asked Carmen Delahunt, who was coordinating the efforts of the Maritime Organization, which had lobbied for a piece of the action, eager to avenge the death of Anthony Tetlock and the other valued agents in the salvage yard firefight.

"They've got a fresh EID team heading up the coast from Sanya as we speak," she reported. "They should be in position by the time Striker's ready to make his move."

"And they know they're strictly backup?"

"On an as-needed basis," the redhead replied. "They're chomping at the bit for some payback, though, so we'll have to see whether they're able to cool their jets and wait things out on the sidelines."

"Speaking of jets," Brognola said, turning to Akira Tokaido, "do we have an ETA for the boys?"

"They went airborne about three minutes ago," Tokaido responded. "Striker's flying with Grimaldi and Cowboy's riding shotgun in the other F-14. I've got them down for reaching the island by the top of the hour."

Hunt Wethers anticipated Brognola's next question and confirmed, "There will be a tour chopper waiting when they get there. Once Cowboy and Striker are dropped off, Jack will refuel and take to the air. The Navy needs the other Tomcat back for some other assignment."

"Jack's confident he can handle his end flying solo?" Brognola asked.

Wethers was perhaps the least humor-prone member of Kurtzman's cyberteam, but he couldn't help but indulge in a smile as he glanced at Brognola. "You know Jack. If he had his druthers, he'd see to it that every assignment wound up with him dogfighting one-on-one with the Red Baron."

Brognola smiled. "I suppose you're right."

Kurtzman saw that his coffeepot was nearly empty. From force of habit, he reached beneath the stand it rested on and started to pull out a bean grinder and fresh filter. He caught himself, however, and put the materials back. Caffeine already had his heart jackrabbiting inside his chest, and he knew over the next hour or so there'd be more than enough adrenaline coursing through his system to ward off any chance of fatigue.

"One thing we haven't taken into consideration," he told Brognola, voicing a concern that had been gnawing at the back of his mind. "What if Li Chuannan turns up before he reaches Ki Dan's little San Simeon? Do we intercept him?"

"Good question," Brognola said. "The party line would be that we grab him first chance we get."

"Yeah, I figured that much," Kurtzman said. "But you know what I'm getting at."

The big Fed didn't have to dwell on the matter long. He knew up front the way things should be handled.

"If we spot him, fine," Brognola said. "Just keep him under surveillance and pass along his coordinates. Unless something goes awry and he forces our hand, let him wander out onto the web, then we'll leave things to the spider."

32

Airspace over South China Sea

Riding behind Jack Grimaldi in the cockpit of the F-14, Bolan looked away from the jet's display console and, for the second time in less than twelve hours, stared down at Hainan Island. Unlike the dark, amorphous landmass he'd scanned the previous night, the island now looked like the tropical paradise that had become a magnet for billions of dollars' worth of Chinese investment capital. He saw throngs of beachgoers clogging stretches of white sand, while sailboats with crisp white sails roamed the gleaming waters. And all along the coast there were developed pockets where resorts rubbed elbows with other upscale properties. One of those properties would be Bolan's ultimate destination.

The Executioner was absorbed by logistical considerations. Since leaving Hong Kong, he'd been in constant contact with the Farm, helping to orchestrate the scenario that would play out once Grimaldi brought the plane down. The word so far was that all systems were go. All that remained to be seen was whether or not the elaborate preparations would pay off. The one missing piece thusfar was irrefutable proof that Jiang Yang and Li Chuannan had indeed shown their faces at Ki Dan's private estate. Bolan had no interest in the billionaire or any criminal wrongdoings he may have been party to while amassing his fortune. Unless it turned out that Ki Dan was holding court with the two San Hop Kwan thugs.

Bolan had the coordinates for Dan's estate, and as Grimaldi began his descent, he turned his attention back to the targeting screens for the F-14's weapons systems. He cued up an image of the mansion and surrounding acreage, then toggled a cursor back and forth, looking for signs of activity. He could see a few gardeners pruning trees and shrubs near the guest homes, and a three-man maintenance crew had drained the hot tub adjacent to the massive swimming pool and were apparently repairing some of the spa's jets.

A narrow asphalt path wound its way through the property, and Bolan counted guards in three separate small electric carts making security rounds. The screen image wasn't clear enough for him to determine how well the guards were armed, but Bolan figured it was a safe bet they were toting submachine guns and side arms. It was also a given that they were in communication with one another by way of walkie-talkies. They would provide a challenge, and Bolan suspected Ki Dan had more goons on the prowl elsewhere on the premises.

Most of the estate was surrounded by a ten-foot-high brick wall mounted at regular intervals with surveillance cameras. In several spots, most notably behind the guesthouses, the terrain was uneven and the barrier was instead comprised of wire mesh topped with rolled barbed wire.

"Not a welcome mat in sight, eh?" Grimaldi said over his headset from the cockpit. He was watching the same display screen as Bolan.

"I didn't expect them to make it easy for us," Bolan replied into his headset, his voice hard. "But once we get word those scumbags are in there, I don't care how many alligators they throw in the moat, I'm going in."

Hainan Island, China

A QUARTER MILE up the access road leading to the Emerald Cotillion Golf Course, a maintenance truck bearing the ECGC logo pulled into a construction lot where the unfinished shell of a two-story building was surrounded by a fresh-laid layer of asphalt. When completed a few months down the line, the building would serve as a low-rent motel for golf patrons wary of coughing up three hundred dollars a night to stay at the course's four-star hotel. There were no workers at the site, and the only other vehicle, an unmarked utility van, was parked behind the building out of sight from the road. There was just enough room for the maintenance truck to pull to a stop alongside the van.

The man driving the truck was not part of the golf course's ground crew, but rather Marc Funaki, the recently hired head of security at ECGC. Funaki, a Japanese American whose primary allegiance was to the U.S. Federal Trade Commission, had moled his way onto the payroll at Cotillion as part of a long-running investigation into allegations of insider trading on the Hong Kong, Tokyo and U.S. stock exchanges by Ki Dan, who was the principal stockholder of ECGC's parent corporation.

Following the phone orders he'd received less than an hour earlier, Funaki got out of the truck and circled back, dropping the tailgate. Moments later, the rear door of the van opened. One by one, seven UNMO-EID commandos in combat fatigues piled out and transferred to the back of the truck, where they would be concealed by the vehicle's fiberglass shell. The men's faces were streaked with combat cosmetics and they were armed with Sigma SW40F autoloaders as well as Parker-Hale IDW 9 mm submachine guns.

"I hope you're going to pick up your divots," the security

chief told the EID team leader, a fifty-year-old Briton by the name of Wesley Aames.

"Bloody well right," Aames deadpanned as he climbed aboard the truck and pulled the tailgate closed behind him. "You know where to take us."

Funaki nodded and got back behind the wheel. Three minutes later he was back at the golf course, following a gravel service road that ran between the eighteenth-hole fairway and the mountain slope leading up to the estate of Ki Dan. Sprinklers were watering the fairway and several other sprinkler heads had been deliberately removed, allowing geyser-like streams to drench the manicured grass. Golfers had been told that vandals had broken the heads and rewired the timers, flooding the fairway for no good reason. Consequently, the eighteenth hole had been shut down for the rest of the day, reducing the chance that someone might spot the UN troops and pass along word to course officials who might, in turn, relay word to Ki Dan.

Halfway down the fairway, the service road passed through a dense cluster of trees extending out from the base of the mountain. Once Funaki had driven into the cover provided by the trees, he put the truck in Park and left the engine running. Aames, meanwhile, dropped the tailgate and led his men out of the truck. Strapping their subguns over their shoulders, the commandos started through the woods, making their way to the base of the mountain. Through a gap in the treetops, Aames could see the obstacle course that lay ahead. The mountainside rose sharply upward from the golf course and, thanks to the regularity of coastal rains, the near-vertical terrain was lush with vegetation.

"How about letting me know why you're raiding Ki Dan's place?" Funaki asked. "I mean, it's not like I don't have a stake in this."

"Confidential, mate," Aames told the man. "All I can tell you is we're after that bloke for something more than trade violations."

"Sounds serious," the security officer said, still fishing.

Aames grinned at Funaki. "That's why we're wearing fatigues instead of tuxedos. Now, if you want to know more, you'll have to wait and turn on the telly for the evening news."

Funaki shrugged, watching the first of Aames's men begin to scale the steep slope. "I may be wrong," he ventured, "but something tells me anything I see on the news is going to be a cover story."

33

Stony Man Farm, Virginia

"The EID team is moving into position," Aaron Kurtzman said, passing on the update he'd just received from Wesley Aames. "They're going to rig the deck pylons with plastique, then after they do the same with a couple of wall sections, they'll take cover and wait on a signal to detonate."

"Should it come to that," Brognola said.

Across the Computer Room, Carmen Delahunt called out, "Striker and Cowboy are in the tour chopper and on the way to their insertion point."

"So far, so good, then," Brognola said. He turned to Huntington Wethers, who, for the past hour, had been focused on the task of monitoring communication frequencies being used by the billionaire's security force. "Any luck on your end?"

"I've got a tap on the phone line so far, but that's it," Wethers said. "I'll keep sniffing around until I get something from their walkie-talkies."

"That'd help," Brognola said.

"Hang on," Tokaido interjected. He'd just refreshed the Satcam feed and had panned to an image of the main entrance to Dan's estate. A nondescript-looking sedan had pulled up to the security gate. "Looks like we have a visitor."

"Seems like the gate folks are using the phone line as a

link to the main house," Wethers called out from his computer station.

He clicked on his software's sound function, routing the phone dispatch through his speakers so the others could listen in as well. There was considerable distortion on the line, but everyone in the room was able to hear the name of the visitor once the guard announced him to Ki Dan.

"Chuannan," Brognola whispered. "Welcome to the party."

Hainan Island, China

THE MOUNTAINS ROLLING inland behind Ki Dan's estate were undeveloped and largely inaccessible and, as such, had been designated as part of the Hainan Island Wildlife Preserve. Those wishing a glimpse of endangered species dwelling on the island—most notably Eld's deer, black gibbons and the rare mottled heron—could either rough it on trails maintained by forest rangers or opt for aerial tours operated by three separate contractors based out of Sanya International Airport and a smaller airport servicing the coastal area near the Feike Resort and Casino.

Bolan and Kissinger had boarded a chopper at the latter location. The tour pilot had been replaced by a UNMO operative, and en route to their drop point, the Stony Man operatives had been assured that Ki Dan was used to helicopters flying over the mountains behind his property. As such, their approach was unlikely to raise any red flags with Dan's security force.

Twenty minutes after taking to the air, Bolan and Kissinger stepped off the chopper, which had set down on a broad escarpment situated on the far side of the mountain overlooking Ki Dan's guesthouses.

"We'll signal you when we need a pickup," Bolan told the pilot, gesturing at the walkie-talkie clipped to his waist.

The pilot nodded. "I'm not going anywhere unless some rhinoceros wanders up here looking to butt heads with me."

Once they'd moved clear of the chopper, Bolan led Kissinger up a ragged trail leading to the mountaintop. Both men were heavily armed. In addition to his Beretta, the Executioner had helped himself to one of the UNMO's Hale-Parker subguns. A sheathed Ka-Bar combat knife was strapped to his right thigh and three grenades were pocketed in the same ammo belt holding his walkie-talkie.

Kissinger's web holster coddled a Colt Government Model 1911, leaving his hands free to grip a sniper rifle with five 7.62 mm rounds tucked into its staggered mag box.

"Looks like your hammy's eased up on you," Kissinger said, noting the relative ease in Bolan's step.

"I'm not about to high-jump in the Olympics," Bolan said, "but I'll manage."

"Hold on a sec," Kissinger said, holding up a hand as he slowed to a stop. He cupped one hand to his ear so that he could better hear the message being radioed to his earphone from Stony Man Farm.

"Perfect timing," he said, as much to Bolan as Akira Tokaido.

"What's up?" Bolan asked.

Kissinger turned to the Executioner. "Li Chuannan just showed up down the hill. Jiang Yang's here, too."

"Then we're in business," Bolan said.

Once they reached the mountaintop, both men dropped to the ground and crawled along the crest until they reached a point where they could look down on Ki Dan's estate.

"Looks even more impressive firsthand," Kissinger said.

Bolan scanned the property until he spotted Li Chuannan's sedan heading up the long driveway leading to the mansion. Reaching to his ammo belt, he unclipped a Nikon 5x15 Monocular HG. The lens was nonreflective, allowing him to look through it without worrying that sunlight might bounce off the glass and tip off his position. He adjusted the focus, bringing the front windshield of the sedan into crisp view. Once he got a good look at the man behind the wheel, he lowered the spyglass.

"It's him, all right," he said.

Kissinger unslung his rifle and brought it into firing position. "Don't worry," he told Bolan, "I won't pull the trigger unless I have to. For now, he's all yours."

"I guess that's my cue."

Bolan set down the spyglass, then crawled away from Kissinger, seeking out a nearby clot of brush.

"Good luck," Kissinger called out to him.

Once Bolan reached the clustered foliage, he took a deep breath, then slowly began to head downhill, using the vegetation for cover. Li Chuannan soon fell out of view, but Bolan knew that was only temporary. Soon enough, he would have Christine Wood's killer back his sights.

LI CHUANNAN GOT OUT of the Lexus GS 300 he'd rented after getting off the ferry and strode up the flagstone walk leading to Ki Dan's mansion. He was empty-handed, having left Hu Dzem's valise in a locker back at the port facilities. The way he looked at it, there was no need to share his plunder. It would be his fallback in case things didn't pan out with the billionaire.

Jiang Yang greeted him at the door with a wide grin.

"I knew I could count on you," Yang told the ex-wrestler.

Li Chuannan shrugged. "Hu Dzem had it coming. He was behind the times."

"Thanks to you, he'll stay that way." Yang laughed. When they'd spoken on the phone shortly after the chairman's murder, the Dai Lo hadn't mentioned the fact that he'd sent Ling Thieu to the Dynasty on the chance Chuannan botched the execution. Yang wasn't about to bring the matter up now, either. While he'd yet to receive any confirmation, Yang suspected that Thieu had died during the mayhem at the brothel. It was best, Yang figured, that the man take the secret to his grave.

Chuannan followed Yang through the foyer into the receiving room, where Ki Dan was wrapping up a call on his cell phone. Chuannan took in the row of framed Picasso drawings lining the wall nearest to him and smirked. "Most people put their kid's artwork on the refrigerator," he said jokingly.

"Probably not a good idea to tell Ki Dan that," Yang advised.

Once the billionaire was off the phone, Yang introduced him to Li Chuannan. Ki Dan did a double-take as he looked at Hu Dzem's killer.

"Juggernaut?" he asked.

Li Chuannan was taken aback. "You're a wrestling fan?"

Dan beamed and offered Chuannan a respectful bow. "I love wrestling!" he said. "As a matter of fact, I almost bought the organization you wrestled for, but I didn't think I could turn a profit. But I loved you as Juggernaut! I always wondered what happened to you."

"It was a job," Chuannan said. "I moved on."

"Of course," Dan said.

Jiang Yang was fast tiring of the small talk. "Now that he's here," he said, "maybe it's time we discussed our arrangement."

"Very well," Dan said. He stared out the nearest window, then told the two gangsters, "It's such a nice day. Let's do this outside. The upstairs terrace has a great view of the sea."

"Fine by me," Yang said.

"Anywhere you want," Li Chuannan agreed.

As he led his guests up the sweeping staircase leading to the second floor, Dan stayed close to Chuannan.

"I have a private gym in the basement," the billionaire said. "Maybe afterward we can go there and you can show me some of your wrestling moves."

"If I can remember them," Chuannan said.

Bringing up the rear, Yang fought back a pang of jealousy. He'd had no idea Ki Dan was so fascinated with wrestling, and he was wary Chuannan might try to exploit the situation.

The bouncer had carried out Hu Dzem's execution, but it was Yang who'd ordered it, Yang who'd schemed to curry favor with Ki Dan so they could opt out of the triad. Was it possible that the billionaire would overlook all this and wind up giving Li Chuannan—a mere functionary—more favorable treatment merely because he'd once pranced around a wrestling ring in leotards? There was no way Yang would stand for such disrespect. If things came to that, Yang was determined to show Ki Dan that Juggernaut was no match for the man they called Skull Face.

Once they reached the second floor, Ki Dan led the men down the hallway to a large ballroom overlooking the terrace. Two of the billionaire's bodyguards were standing outside, and when they saw Dan approaching with the two gangsters, one of them opened the French doors leading to the elevated patio.

"I'll be right with you," Dan told Yang and Chuannan, gesturing them outside. "I have a small business matter to attend to first."

The gangsters moved out onto the terrace, a tiled, open-air area the size of a tennis court. Dan asked them what they would like to drink, then took his guards aside once they'd joined him in the ballroom.

"Give me a few minutes to see what kind of useful information they might have," he told them, "then bring out their drinks along with something that looks like important paperwork that needs my signature. When I take my pen out, that will be your signal."

"To kill them," one of the guards said.

"Yes," Dan said. "Hu Dzem will be needing some associates to boss around in hell."

34

Mack Bolan reached the bottom of the mountain without incident. His hamstring was protesting the strain put on it, but the Executioner had more pressing concerns. He sized up the section of thick wire fencing that stood between him and Ki Dan's estate. The same rampant growth of ivy that provided his cover also obstructed the nearest surveillance camera, further blocking him from view of anyone inside the multimillion-dollar compound.

Bolan pried his fingers through the dense leaves, creating a small opening in what had become a nearly solid wall of vegetation. Peering through the opening, he could see wide expanse of back lawn shared by the three guesthouses. There was no one about, and when he saw that the shades were all drawn in each of the homes, the Executioner guessed that if anyone besides Jiang Yang and Li Chuannan were visiting, Ki Dan was putting them up at the mansion. Still, Bolan was determined to make as little noise as possible.

Reaching into his rear pocket, the Executioner took out a small, pronged instrument that looked like a palm-sized Taser gun. A similar contraption had helped him and the UN troops gain access to the salvage yard in Jotuwi. Straddling the prongs on either side of a length of the fence's wire mesh, Bolan thumbed a switch set into the handle. As the prongs closed in on each other, Bolan could feel the heat they were generating as they warmed the wire. When a signal light on the palm grip changed from red to green, a pair of retractable, titanium-edged blades emerged from inside the prongs, cutting quietly through the weakened wire. Bolan was once impressed with the bolt cutters dreamed up by Able Team's mechanical wizard Gadgets Schwarz.

It took the Executioner less than two minutes to create an opening large enough to squeeze through. Once he was on the other side, he wasted no time clearing the swath of lawn and taking cover behind an outdoor barbecue located near the far end of the middle house. He took a moment to catch his breath and make sure his entry had gone undetected, then grabbed his walkie-talkie and clicked through to Kissinger.

"I'm in," he said.

"I know," Kissinger replied through Bolan's earbud. "I can see you."

"Good," Bolan whispered back. "What's it look like between here and the mansion?"

"Well, first the good news," Kissinger reported. "Your guys just stepped out onto a terrace off the second story. They're sitting down, and if they stay put you won't have to go inside looking for them."

"Does there have to be bad news?" Bolan said.

"Always. There's a guard in one of those electric golf carts taking a cigarette break with a couple gardeners on your side of the botanical garden. There's no cover between you and them, so you won't be able to sneak up on them. They'd have to be blind to miss you once you move away from the guesthouses."

"I can't afford to wait them out," Bolan said.

"Like I said, bad news," Kissinger said. "I could take the guard out for you, but the gardeners would probably spread the alarm before I could get to them. I know you've got a suppressor on the Beretta, but I don't trust the range you're dealing with."

"Neither do I," Bolan said. He quickly weighed his options. The grenades he'd brought along were as useless in this situation as his Beretta or the subgun slung over his shoulder. He'd hoped to hold his other trump cards a little deeper into the game, but it seemed as if he had no choice but to play them.

"We'll have to go with some diversion," he told Kissinger. "Are you linked up with the EID squad?"

"Yeah," Kissinger told him. "They've reached the top of the cliff and are rigging the plastique. All they'll need is the green light and the wall comes tumbling down. Or at least enough of it to let them onto the grounds."

"Go ahead and give them the green light," Bolan said, slipping the Beretta free of its web holster. "And while you're at it, see if Jack's got something on that Tomcat he can throw down to make sure Yang and Chuannan stay put on the terrace until I can get to them."

ONCE HE'D SECURED A SLAB of plastique to a portion of the clifftop wall, Wesley Aames scrambled downhill, joining another member of the EID team.

"All set," he said.

"Be a shame for us to go to all this trouble and not follow through," the other commando groused. "I don't see why we should have to hang back and let some outsider hog all the action."

"Office politics, lad," Aames responded. "Ours is not to reason why."

The commando glanced at the surrounding vegetation, eyeing the other stormtroopers positioned near the top of the cliff. He was about to press Aames to allow them to carry out their part of the plan unilaterally when the Briton turned away from him, fielding a call on his walkie-talkie. Aames whispered into the receiver, then clicked the communicator off and turned back to his colleague, grinning.

"Do what?" Jack Grimaldi exclaimed through his headset once he'd fielded Kissinger's request. He was thirty thousand feet up and ten nautical miles from Ki Dan's estate, but thanks to the sensors feeding his HUD, he had a clear view of the mansion.

"Sorry, Cowboy," he said, "but I'm fresh out of long-range Molotovs. From up here I can hit the balcony doors with another GBU, no problem, but there's no guarantee anything will be left standing. And if the shrapnel doesn't kill those guys, having the terrace give out from under them will. No can do, compadre."

"I was afraid you were going to say that," Kissinger replied.

"If you can buy some time, I'll scoot down with the chattergun," Grimaldi offered. "Let me get within a mile and I can do a strafing run that'll make 'em think twice about going inside. Of course, the Vulcan's not keen on finesse, so it's not like I can stitch the doors. One stray round and we're back to Striker stumbling across bodies that look like Swiss cheese."

"We'll have to take our chances," Kissinger said. "Head on down, but be ready to abort on my signal."

"Roger."

Grimaldi ended the call and dipped one wing, dropping the F-14 into a quick descent toward a veil of clouds. He let his gaze drift to the controls for the Tomcat's A-1 Vulcan rotary cannon, a glorified upgrade of the Civil War Gatling gun housed in the fuselage below his seat. The A-1 was good for a muzzle velocity of 3600 feet per second and 6000 rounds of chain-fed 20 mm ammunition per minute, but asking it to perform the task Grimaldi had been presented with was like asking someone to core apples with a tommygun.

"Find another way, Sarge," he murmured, "'cause I don't wanna spoil the party."

Slaughter House

"ENOUGH ABOUT THE TRIADS," Yang grumbled as he shifted position in his patio chair. "I thought we were going to talk about your operations and where we could fit in."

"Of course," Ki Dan replied as he refilled Yang's glass with champagne. He'd spent the past few minutes testing the Dai Lo's patience with questions about San Kwan Hop's inner workings, but neither Yang nor Chuannan had been forthcoming with information the billionaire wasn't already aware of. As such, they'd outlived their usefulness to him. It was time to set them up for the kill.

"Now then," he said, "why don't you both tell me what kind of work you'd like to be doing and we can take it from there."

"Not wrestling, I can tell you that much right off the top," Li Chuannan said, half-smiling.

The billionaire smiled back.

"Understood," he said. "But consider this. What if I were to go ahead and buy your old wrestling league and turn it over to you? Wouldn't you maybe like the opportunity to be giving orders to the same people who were once giving them to you?"

Li Chuannan thought about it as he sipped his champagne. "Since you put it that way..." he said. "There might be something to that."

"We don't need to rush into anything," Dan told him. "You can take some time to think it over."

"I'll do that," Chuannan said.

Jiang Yang stared at his colleague with disbelief. A wrestling promotion? Was Li Chuannan really that lacking in ambition? So eager to be paid off with a mere pittance compared to what he could get if he bothered to negotiate a little harder? Yang felt himself losing respect for the one-time grappler. At the same time, he felt relief. There clearly wasn't going to be any tug-of-war between them in terms of seeing who came out ahead once they were officially on board with Ki Dan.

"What about you?" the businessman asked Yang. "You've

been so anxious to get into this, I'm sure you've thought out some options for yourself."

Now we're finally getting somewhere, Yang thought. "You just took over a film production company in Beijing," he told the billionaire, launching into the proposal he'd been running through his mind ever since he first entered into a partnership with Ki Dan. "In the papers you said you wanted to turn it into China's answer to a Hollywood studio. One of the bigger ones."

Ki Dan nodded indulgently. From the corner of his eye he saw his two bodyguards coming out onto the terrace, one holding a manila folder, the other wheeling a service tray piled high with pastries, coffee and bowls of fresh fruit. For Ki Dan, their timing couldn't have been better.

"You've done your homework," he told Yang. "I'm impressed."

Yang pretended to ignore the compliment. "I could see myself running that studio," he said.

Ki Dan raised an eyebrow. "Really? You mean to say you'd prefer all that tiresome glamour, womanizing and partying over the kind of work you're more used to? What's the matter, don't you like waking up every morning wondering if you'll live through the day?"

"I know that part will be hard to give up," Yang said, his voice filled with sarcasm. "But what can I say? I'm ready for a new challenge."

"Obviously." Ki Dan turned to his bodyguards and pretended to be upset by their arrival. "I thought I gave orders that we were not to be disturbed."

"My apologies, sir," the man with the paperwork said, "but there's been a snag in the merger talks you were discussing in the Philippines last night. We received word that you need to sign some disclosure forms."

"And the chef had already put this together," the other guard said, gesturing at the food spread, "so I thought I might as well bring it out."

"Very well." Ki Dan sighed. As he took the paperwork, he told the men, "As long as you're out here, can you bring over one of the umbrellas? The glare is getting to be a bit much."

The guards nodded and moved away from Ki Dan, circling behind Jiang Yang and Li Chuannan to gain access to a large wooden receptacle holding several large canvas patio umbrellas.

Li Chuannan glanced over his shoulder at them, then turned back once he saw them fitting one of the umbrellas into a stand and unfurling the canvas. As they went about their task, the guards kept an eye on Ki Dan, waiting on his signal to carry out the execution of the San Hop Kwan members.

As he scanned the paperwork, Ki Dan told Yang, "I hope you realize that if you're running a studio, you'll spend more time doing things like this than running around with starlets."

"I can live with that," Yang replied.

"Well," Dan said, setting the papers on the table in front of him and reaching for his pen, "everything seems to be in order."

Signal given, the two guards stopped what they were doing and moved away from the half-opened umbrella, both reaching inside their suit jackets for silencer-equipped Heckler & Koch Mk.23 pistols, Ki Dan's weapon of choice for his security detail.

Before either man could withdraw their handguns, however, an unexpected chorus of explosions rocked the grounds with so much force the terrace quaked and sent the men staggering into one another. Suddenly the executions had been put on hold.

BOLAN FELT THE GROUND tremble beneath him, but he'd been prepared for the explosions. Losing no time, he burst from cover between the guest homes and ran as swiftly as his hamstring would allow. As he'd hoped, the blasts set by the EID stormtroopers had drawn the attention of the security guard as well as the gardeners. They had their backs turned to him as they strained to see past the botanical gardens. The guard sensed Bolan's approach and turned as the Executioner was less than twenty yards away. Bolan was able to fire first, dropping the guard with a 3-round kill shot to the chest.

As the gunman went down, Bolan turned his Beretta on the gardeners, hoping the mere sight of the gun would take them out of the equation. Both gardeners ran for the shelter of the botanical gardens.

The Executioner crouched over the slain guard. The man's uniform coat had been bloodied from the shots he'd taken, but Bolan pulled it free anyway and shoved his arms through the sleeves, then grabbed the guard's hat before climbing behind the controls of the golf cart.

As he was setting the Parker-Hale subgun on the bench seat beside him, Bolan heard the crackle of the dead man's walkie-talkie. Whoever was trying to reach the guard was speaking frantically in Chinese, and Bolan couldn't make out what was being said. It didn't matter. The Executioner's only concern was to reach the terrace as quickly as possible and hope his haphazard disguise would hold up for the duration.

Bolan floored the accelerator, but the cart's top speed was less than twenty miles an hour and it felt as if he was crawling as he drove around the outer edge of the botanical gardens. The huge pool was directly ahead, and the workers he'd seen earlier while aboard the jet were scrambling out of the hot tub, trying to figure out what was happening. One of the men turned toward Bolan and opened his mouth as if to speak. He caught himself, however, once he saw that it wasn't one of the guards behind the wheel of the cart. The man shouted to his colleagues, and soon all three men were setting aside their tools in favor of handguns.

Bolan had no time to get caught up in a protracted gunfight. Taking one hand from the wheel, he grabbed one of his grenades and freed the pin, then slung the bomb underhanded in the direction of the pool. The grenade detonated on the concrete pool decking a few yards in front of the workers, hurtling enough shrapnel and concrete shards to bring the men down. Bolan made sure none of the rose back to their feet, then floored the cart again and continued toward the mansion.

35

"What the hell is going on!" Ki Dan raged, vaulting from his chair and stepping over the glass shards of the champagne glass he'd dropped when the explosions had taken him by surprise.

Jiang Yang and Li Chuannan were on their feet, too. The terrace had stopped trembling and they stared past the stone railing, along with the billionaire and his bodyguards, at wisps of smoke rising from the far side of the distant wall separating the estate from the steep drop-off to the golf course. The observation deck had vanished from view, and armed commandos could be seen scrambling through charred gaps in the brick wall.

Dan's security force was headed toward the wall, some on foot while others powered their electric carts into battle. At first glance it seemed as if the numbers were even, but the billionaire doubted his men could withstand an assault by trained commandos. As the two sides began to exchange gunfire, Ki Dan turned on Jiang Yang, eyes flaring with accusation.

"You!" he shouted. "You're behind this!"

"No!" Yang retorted, confused.

Ki Dan saw no point in arguing the matter. He turned on his heel and started for the French doors leading inside the mansion, shouting over his shoulders to his bodyguards, "What are you waiting for? Kill them!"

The guards, finally recovered from the sudden turn of events, once again went for their pistols. Neither Yang nor

Slaughter House

Chuannan were armed, but both men had heard Ki Dan's command and were quick to react. Yang shoved the pastry cart across the terrace tiles, striking one guard in the shins. Chuannan, meanwhile, grabbed hold of the wrought-iron chair he'd been sitting on and charged the other gunman. The second guard managed to get off a shot, but it glanced off the chair's sturdy frame, missing its mark.

As Juggernaut, Li Chuannan had delivered his share of chair shots in the wrestling ring, but in those instances he'd used folding chairs that had caused little harm to his opponents. This was different. The solid chair's iron leg struck the guard's forearm with so much force it shattered the man's ulna bone. The gunman howled, dropping his gun. Chuannan kicked the gun aside and delivered a second blow with the chair, catching the guard's neck just below the base of his skull. The man's howling ceased as the impact of the blow sent him crashing to the tiles, unconscious.

By then Yang had dived over the pastry cart and tackled the first guard. The guard still had his gun, but Yang was fighting him for it. Chuannan was about to lend a hand when he heard a shot and felt a bullet ram into his right thigh. He let out a yelp and glanced back at Ki Dan, who'd drawn an H&K of his own and was standing just outside the half-opened door leading back into the mansion. The gun was pointed at Chuannan's chest.

"I have to do everything myself," the billionaire muttered.

Dan was about to pull the trigger when the glass behind him suddenly shattered. Thundering 20 mm rounds from Jack Grimaldi's distant cannon shredded an overhead awning and punched holes through the wall itself, showering Dan with debris.

The billionaire had been spared any direct hits, but Li Chuannan remedied the situation once he got his hands on the stray pistol. "Here, wrestle with this!" he shouted as he took aim at Dan and pulled the trigger.

Dan dropped to his knees, struggling to return fire. Chuannan wasn't about to give him the opportunity. He pumped two more rounds into the billionaire, insuring that once he went down he would stay that way. Then he turned back to lend a hand to his colleague.

Yang was still fighting to get hold of the first guard's H&K, but the other man had better leverage and finally yanked his arm free of Yang's grasp. His victory was short-lived, however, as Chuannan moved in and coldcocked him with the butt of his pistol, then put a round into his skull.

"You're getting good at this," Yang told Chuannan as the ex-wrestler helped him to his feet.

"Yeah, we're fine for the moment," Chuannan responded, "but what do we do now?"

"Inside!" Yang shouted, heading toward the cannon-ravaged entryway where Ki Dan lay sprawled amid shattered glass and debris.

Chuannan began to follow, but both men stopped short as another volley of Tomcat hellfire tore into the would-be escape route. Seconds later, a thundering in the heavens announced the arrival of Jack Grimaldi's F-14. The fighter jet was flying in low over the South China Sea, on a course that would soon bring it roaring over the grounds of the estate.

Yang turned from the mansion and stared at the jet, then out past the terrace at the squad of commandos who had quickly overwhelmed the rest of Ki Dan's security detail. The few guards who hadn't been gunned down in the initial exchange had cast aside their weapons and raised their hands in surrender.

Yang, however, wasn't about to join them. He glanced around and spotted a staircase leading down to the grounds. It looked to him as if the steps might be shielded from the view of the men who'd broken through the wall near the cliff. If so, he figured he and Chuannan might be able to circle around the mansion undetected.

"There has to be a back way," he told Chuannan as he

broke for the steps, detouring long enough to retrieve Ki Dan's pistol. "Let's get out of here!"

The shadow of the F-14 swept across the terrace. Yang and Chuannan followed its course to the marbled staircase and started down. Yang took the steps two at a time, but Chuannan was slowed by the gunshot wound to his thigh. He left a trail of blood on the steps and railing he used for support.

"Hurry!" Yang whispered hoarsely.

"I've been shot, damn it!" Chuannan protested.

Once the bouncer caught up with Yang, they stayed close to the mansion, trodding through flowerbeds and sidestepping a planter box filled with hedges meticulously trimmed into the shape of various animals. No one had spotted them yet, and the closer they came to the corner that would take them around to the side grounds, the more Yang began to feel that he might yet again elude his pursuers.

There was one contingency the gangster hadn't anticipated, however.

Just as Yang and Chuannan rounded a trimmed green dolphin rising up from the last planter in front of the house, the two triad defectors found their way blocked by a security cart that was slowing to a stop directly before them. Yang's gaze locked on that of the man behind the wheel, and in that fleeting moment the gangster knew he'd stumbled into hell.

IT WASN'T THE WAY BOLAN had envisioned confronting his prey, but once he recognized Yang and Chuannan and saw that both men were armed, he promptly forgot about all the other scenarios. Improvising, he went on the offensive, shifting his foot from the brake back to the accelerator. The cart lurched forward, Bolan jerking the steering wheel, veering toward the two foot gap between the two men. Instead of a direct hit, Bolan managed to clip them both simultaneously with enough force to knock them off balance. Chuannan was hit more squarely and his knees buckled as he toppled backward, arms flailing. He struck his head against the carved stonework framing one of the lower windows and lost consciousness. A lush bed of fiery orange nasturtiums broke his fall and his gun fell from view amid the maze of bright-colored petals.

Yang fared better. His instincts had nearly matched Bolan's, and he was able roll with the impact of the cart and scramble quickly to his feet, still clutching his pistol.

The cart was still rolling when Bolan leaped clear and charged the Dai Lo. When he saw Yang raising his gun, he veered and torqued his body, lashing out with a left-legged karate kick. The blow struck Yang's gun hand squarely, forcing him to drop the pistol. The move, however, put more strain on Bolan's injured hamstring than his protective sheathing could compensate for, and he grimaced as a blinding white flash of pain raced through his entire body, forcing him to one knee. Teeth clenched, fighting back the pain, he still managed to draw bead on Yang with his Beretta.

"Don't move!" he commanded.

Yang froze in midcrouch, one arm extended toward his fallen handgun. He glared at Bolan, a glimmer of recognition coming to his eyes. With it came a rush of anger.

"Jotuwi," the skull-faced gangster grated. "It was you by the river!"

"That's right." Bolan winced as he rose. "And when you fled I followed you to the salvage yard. From there, I followed you in your jet, and once I found out where you parachuted, I followed you here. Now the chase is over."

"Who are you?" Yang demanded to know. "Who do you work for?"

"It doesn't matter," Bolan told the man. "I'm your judge and your jury. I'm your executioner."

Yang was only half-listening. Bolan saw the man's eyes rove to the flower bed where Chuannan had fallen. When he heard a rustling in the nasturtiums, Bolan abruptly swung around.

Chuannan was on his feet. The blow to his head had left a knot that had already swollen to the size of an egg, but the bouncer wasn't about to be stopped by the injury any more than he'd been slowed by the bullet lodged in his thigh. He pushed off his wounded leg and dived headlong at Bolan.

The soldier barely had time to lower his head and raise his shoulder before Chuannan was on him. He absorbed the larger man's weight and turned the momentum against him, propelling him over his shoulder.

Chuannan had weathered similar falls countless times in the ring and he reflexively flattened his back, dispersing the force of his landing on the grass. Someone less experienced would likely have had the wind knocked from his lungs, but Chuannan was only briefly stunned.

Jiang Yang, meanwhile, took advantage of Chuannan's assault and lunged toward his fallen pistol, snatching it up cleanly, hand closing around the grip, index finger curling around the trigger. He quickly brought the gun around, hoping to get off a shot while Bolan was still preoccupied. The ploy was futile, however. Before Yang could squeeze the trigger, the Executioner whirled and cut loose with his Beretta, rendering three 9 mm verdicts into the Dai Lo's chest.

Yang staggered backward, his final expression a mixture of hatred and disbelief. Destiny had abandoned him. The life went out of his eyes in the time it took his pistol to drop from his fingers to the grass. When his legs gave out, he backed into the security cart, which had stalled on the grass behind him, then slumped to one side and collapsed.

There was no time for Bolan to savor his victory. Li Chuannan was once again on his feet. A second time the gangster dived Bolan's way, this time lowering his trajectory, eyes fixed on the Executioner's Beretta. Bolan was unable to deflect Chuannan, and before he could get off a shot, the bouncer's massive fingers were clamped around his wrist.

Chuannan fed on his steroid rage. With almost inhuman

strength, he twisted Bolan's arm, forcing him to release the gun, then placed him in a wrestler's version of a half nelson. Bolan grunted in agony as he felt his arm being wrenched behind his back at an unnatural angle. If Chuannan kept up the pressure, Bolan was sure his arm would be ripped free from its socket, immobilizing him. To make matters worse, Chuannan was leaning into him in such a way that Bolan's weight shifted onto his bad leg. The resulting pain was excruciating.

Bolan's vision began to cloud with sparks. He knew that unless he acted fast, he was likely to pass out, in which case there would be little likelihood of his ever regaining consciousness.

Bolan flailed at Chuannan with his free hand, striking at the other man's skull, but there was no force behind the blows and they did little but fan Chuannan's rage, especially when one of the blows glanced off the tender welt left by his earlier fall.

Chuannan let out a prolonged howl, at first steeped in pain, then anticipation. Realizing he had the upper hand, the gangster applied still more brute strength to his submission hold, at the same time bearing his full weight down on Bolan, forcing the Executioner back to his knees. Chuannan wanted his adversary dead, but first he wanted to inflict as much pain as possible. He wanted Bolan to surrender and beg for mercy. After that, Chuannan would kill the man.

The bouncer may have thought he was in control, but even in his weakened state, Bolan was playing Chuannan, looking for an opportunity to press the larger man's strength to his own advantage. With Chuannan about to bend him to the breaking point, Bolan had no choice but to make his move.

After one last ineffectual swat to Chuannan's head, the Executioner dropped his arm to his side and reached past his ammo belt to his thigh. There, still tucked in its sheath, was his combat knife. He gripped the hilt and slid the knife free, then suddenly allowed himself to go limp.

Chuannan, who'd clenched his legs and braced himself so that he could continue to lean his weight into Bolan, instead found himself suddenly flat-footed and unable to keep his balance. Toppling forward, he landed atop Bolan, still clinging to him but now more out of reflex than as part of any strategy.

Bolan felt a ripping sensation as his deltoid muscle tore under the sudden increase in pressure on it by the gangster's lock hold. It was a small sacrifice, however, because the maneuver allowed him enough leverage to put added force into the thrust with which he brought the combat knife's blade stabbing upward into Chuannan's back.

Chuannan screamed and released Bolan as he rolled to one side, pulling himself free of the knife. The soldier still had a firm grip on the weapon, however, and, gasping for breath, he went in for the kill. This time he rammed the serrated blade into the other man's chest, directly below the sternum—the same place where, hours earlier, he'd placed his palms when trying, in vain, to resuscitate Christine Wood with CPR. Once he'd buried the blade to the hilt, Bolan twisted it, ravaging Chuannan's internal organs as he sought out the gangster's heart.

Chuannan snarled at Bolan, trying to fight him off, but blood began to bubble up through his lips and the fight went out of him. His eyes remained open but glazed over, lifeless gaze fixed on the man who now loomed over him, barely conscious himself. Bolan leaned his full weight into the knife a moment longer, then released his grip and collapsed onto the lawn, drained. Bleary-eyed, he stared past the blades of grass at the men he'd just slain.

As he had vowed, Bolan had avenged the deaths of Christine Wood, Anthony Tetlock and all the others killed during the twelve-hour bloodbath that had begun in Malaysia and wound up in the heart of an island paradise.

But vengeance gave him no feeling of euphoria or exultation, anymore than it had the countless other times he'd dispensed it on other foes and adversaries. What he felt instead, was a hollow, fleeting sense of closure. Yes, he'd finished one more chapter in the book he called his War Everlasting, but he knew that soon enough the page would turn and he would find that the war had begun all over again.

To meet that thankless challenge, he knew he would have to take the time to mend, to mourn the dead and regain his strength, to yet again harden his heart and steel his resolution. How long that might take he could not say for sure, but his body told him it was time for the process to begin, and, even as he heard footsteps announcing the approach of Wesley Aames and John Kissinger, Bolan felt the arms of darkness reach out to him. Closing his eyes, he fell into its embrace.

Epilogue

Stony Man Farm, Virginia

As Jack Grimaldi guided the Bell helicopter and began his descent, Hal Brognola finished his cell phone call and turned to Mack Bolan.

"The President says Scott Kelmin sends his regards," the big Fed said. "He says thanks to you, his daughter's back home and has a second chance at things."

Bolan nodded. "How is Eva?"

"As well as can be expected," Brognola said. "She's already met with a therapist and is talking about going back to school."

"Good for her. Let's hope she sticks with it."

Glancing out the window, the Executioner saw a few of the Farm's blacksuits standing near the camouflaged runway where they would soon be landing. Barbara Price was with them, staring up at the approaching helicopter.

"She wanted to come with us to pick you up," Brognola told Bolan, "but Phoenix Force had its hands full in Bali and she needed to stick around and help Bear do some long-distance quarterbacking."

"Business before pleasure," Bolan murmured.

"Something like that," Brognola said.

Moments later, the chopper set down on the runway. It was

a smooth landing, but even the slight jarring was enough to send a fresh jolt of pain coursing through Bolan. His right arm was in a sling and his bad leg was encased in a fiberglass cast. The doctors who'd treated him in China had told it'd be several weeks before he could begin rehabilitation, and the second opinion he'd just gotten at Walter Reed Hospital hadn't been any more promising. Still, the prognosis was that, given time, both his hamstring and deltoid would heal completely. For the time being, though, he was under orders to stay off his feet, and once Grimaldi had shut off the Bell's engines, he emerged from the cockpit and untethered a wheelchair strapped to the cabin wall.

"Okay, Ironside," Grimaldi said, joking, unfolding the chair and wheeling it over to Bolan, "hop on the rolling throne here and we'll get your sorry ass down to terra firma."

"Sure thing, nurse," Bolan shot back.

With some difficulty, he made his way from the passenger seat to the wheelchair, then allowed Grimaldi to push him to the cabin doorway. Brognola had already opened the door, and the blacksuits were positioning the same ramp Aaron Kurtzman relied on when he needed to make use of the chopper.

Once everyone had exited the plane, there was an exchange of greetings with Price, then Grimaldi and Brognola excused themselves, leading the blacksuits away so Bolan and the Farm's mission controller could be alone.

"Welcome back, soldier," Price said.

"Nice to be home," Bolan replied. "My compliments to the reception committee."

"You look like hell," Price said, still smiling.

"I know," Bolan conceded. "Fortunately, it's a few weeks before they take yearbook pictures."

"And I'm going to see to it that you follow doctor's orders those few weeks," Price warned Bolan.

Bolan grinned. "As long as you're so intent on pushing me around, how about getting me from here to the nearest bed?"

Price moved behind the wheelchair and placed her hands on the rear grips. "Relax and enjoy the ride, mister," she said. "That's an order."

JAMES AXLER
DEATH LANDS
Shatter Zone

In this raw, brutal world ruled by the strongest and the most vicious, an unseen player is manipulating Ryan and his band, luring him across an unseen battle line drawn in the dust outside Tucson, Arizona. Here a local barony becomes the staging ground for a battle unlike any other, against a foe whose ties to preDark society present a new and incalculable threat to a fragile world. Ryan Cawdor is the only man living who stands between this adversary's glory...and the prize he seeks.

Available September 2006 wherever you buy books.

Or order your copy now by sending your name, address, zip or postal code, along with a check or money order (please do not send cash) for $6.50 for each book ordered ($7.99 in Canada), plus 75¢ postage and handling ($1.00 in Canada), payable to Gold Eagle Books, to:

In the U.S.
Gold Eagle Books
3010 Walden Avenue
P.O. Box 9077
Buffalo, NY 14269-9077

In Canada
Gold Eagle Books
P.O. Box 636
Fort Erie, Ontario
L2A 5X3

Please specify book title with your order.
Canadian residents add applicable federal and provincial taxes.

GDL75

TAKE 'EM FREE
2 action-packed novels plus a mystery bonus
NO RISK
NO OBLIGATION TO BUY

SPECIAL LIMITED-TIME OFFER

Mail to: Gold Eagle Reader Service™

IN U.S.A.:	IN CANADA:
3010 Walden Ave.	P.O. Box 609
P.O. Box 1867	Fort Erie, Ontario
Buffalo, NY 14240-1867	L2A 5X3

YEAH! Rush me 2 FREE Gold Eagle® novels and my FREE mystery bonus. If I don't cancel, I will receive 6 hot-off-the-press novels every other month. Bill me at the low price of just $29.94* for each shipment. That's a savings of over 10% off the combined cover prices and there is NO extra charge for shipping and handling! There is no minimum number of books I must buy. I can always cancel at any time simply by returning a shipment at your cost or by returning any shipping statement marked "cancel." Even if I never buy another book from Gold Eagle, the 2 free books and mystery bonus are mine to keep forever.

166 ADN DZ76
366 ADN DZ77

Name	(PLEASE PRINT)	
Address		Apt. No.
City	State/Prov.	Zip/Postal Code

Signature (if under 18, parent or guardian must sign)

Not valid to present Gold Eagle® subscribers.
Want to try two free books from another series? Call 1-800-873-8635.

* Terms and prices subject to change without notice. Sales tax applicable in N.Y. Canadian residents will be charged applicable provincial taxes and GST. This offer is limited to one order per household. All orders subject to approval.

® are trademarks owned and used by the trademark owner and or its licensee.

© 2004 Harlequin Enterprises Ltd.

GE-04R

a priceless artifact sparks a quest to keep untold power from the wrong hands...

ROGUE ANGEL

Alex Archer
SOLOMON'S JAR

Rumors of the discovery of Solomon's Jar—in which the biblical King Solomon bound the world's demons after using them to build his temple in Jerusalem—are followed with interest by Annja Creed. Her search leads her to a confrontation with a London cult driven by visions of new world order; and a religious zealot fueled by insatiable glory. Across the sands of the Middle East to the jungles of Brazil, Annja embarks on a relentless chase to stop humanity's most unfathomable secrets from reshaping the modern world.

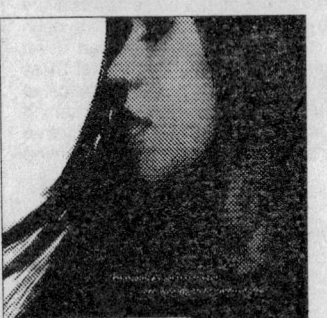

Available September 2006 wherever you buy books.

Genesee District Libraries
Flushing Area Library
120 N. Maple St.
Flushing, MI 48433

GRA2